AN UNFORTUNATE
WOMAN

AN UNFORTUNATE
WOMAN

A Journey

RICHARD BRAUTIGAN

St. Martin's Press ❧ New York

Excerpts from *Iphigenia in Aulis* from *Euripides IV: Four Tragedies: Rhesus,
The Suppliant Women, and Iphigenia in Aulis,* translated by Charles R. Walker.
Copyright © 1958 by the University of Chicago Press.
All rights reserved. Used by permission.

ISBN 0-312-26243-4

First published in France by Bourgois Christian under the title
Cahier d'un retour de troie.

First U.S. Edition: May 2000

10   9   8   7   6   5   4   3   2   1

Iphigenia

> A new home you make for me, Father
> Where will it be?

Agamemnon

> Now stop—it's not right
> For a girl to know all of these things.

Iphigenia

> Father, over there when you have done
> All things well, hurry back to me from Troy!

> EURIPIDES,
> *Iphigenia in Aulis*

N . . .

Dear N,

After I got the telephone call from your friend, I was of course deeply shocked, stunned would be a better word. I just sat beside the telephone for a few moments, staring at it, and then I called a close neighbor M and asked her if she wanted some watermelon. I had bought a watermelon a few days ago for some company, and we didn't get around to eating it, so there I was, a bachelor stuck with too much watermelon.

My neighbor said she would like some watermelon. Why didn't I bring it over in half an hour and have dinner with her and a friend T who was visiting.

I said, I think because of your friend's telephone call, "I'll just bring it over now." I think I probably just wanted to see somebody at that exact moment.

"OK," my neighbor said.

"I'll be right over," I said.

I went to the icebox and got the watermelon and walked over to my neighbor's house, which is just a short distance down the road. I knocked on her kitchen screen door. It took a minute or so for her to answer it. She came downstairs from her bedroom.

"Here's the watermelon," I said, putting it on the kitchen counter.

"Yes," she said, her voice obviously very distant and her physical presence hesitant.

There was something I wanted to show her about the watermelon that required her to get a knife and cut into the melon. It's not important what I wanted to show her about the watermelon, which after doing so, she continued to be hesitant, as if she were someplace else, not actually there in the kitchen with me.

I wanted to talk to her for a few moments about the telephone call that I had gotten from your friend, but then suddenly her hesitancy and growing uncomfortableness made me feel hesitant and uncomfortable.

Finally, I guess, only a couple of minutes had passed and then she said, looking down at the floor, "I left T upstairs writhing around on the bed."

T was a man.

My bringing over the watermelon had just interrupted their lovemaking. My first thoughts were: Why had she answered the telephone while she was making love to somebody and then why didn't she think up some excuse for me not to come over at that time? I mean, she could have said anything and I would have come over later, but instead she had said yes to my coming over.

Anyway, I apologized and went back home.

Then I thought about the humor in the situation and wanted to call you on the telephone and tell you what had just happened because you have the perfect sense of humor to understand it. It's just the kind of story you would have enjoyed and responded to with your musically screeching laughter and said something like "Oh, no!" while still laughing.

I sat there staring at the telephone, wanting very much to call you, but I was completely unable to do so because the telephone call I had gotten from your friend a little while before told me that you had died Thursday.

I had gone over to my friend's house to talk about it when I interrupted her lovemaking. The watermelon was just some kind of funny excuse to talk about my grief and try to get some perspective on the fact that I can never call you again on the telephone and tell you something like I've just done that basically only your sense of humor could appreciate.

Love,

R

NIKKI ARAI DIED OF A HEART ATTACK
ON JULY 8, 1982, IN SAN FRANCISCO
AFTER STRUGGLING AGAINST CANCER
UNTIL HER HEART JUST STOPPED
BEATING. SHE WAS THIRTY-EIGHT.
I SURE AM GOING TO MISS HER.

AN UNFORTUNATE
WOMAN

I saw a brand-new woman's shoe lying in the middle of a quiet Honolulu intersection. It was a brown shoe that sparkled like a leather diamond. There was no apparent reason for the shoe to be lying there such as it playing a part among the leftover remnants of an automobile accident and there were no signs that a parade had passed that way, so the story behind the shoe will never be known.

Did I mention, of course I didn't, that the shoe had no partner? The shoe was alone, solitary, almost haunting. Why is it that when people see one shoe, they almost feel uncomfortable if a second is not about? They look for it. Where is the other shoe? It must be around here someplace.

With this auspicious beginning, I'll continue describing one person's journey, a sort of free fall calendar map, that starts out what seems like years ago, but has actually been just a few months in physical time.

I left Montana in late September, going down to San Francisco for two weeks, and then went back East to Buffalo, New York, to give a lecture, followed by a week in Canada. I returned to San Francisco, where I spent three weeks before being forced by dwindling finances to move across the bay to Berkeley.

I stayed in Berkeley for three weeks, and then went up to Ketchikan, Alaska, for a few days, then flew north to spend the night in Anchorage. The next morning, very early, I left the snow of Anchorage and flew to Honolulu (please bear with me while I finish this calendar map), Hawaii, where I spent a month, taking two days around the middle of my stay there to go to the island of Maui. Then I went back to Honolulu, where I finished out my visit, returning from there to Berkeley, where I'm living now, waiting to go to Chicago in the middle of February.

Now that we have some rough idea of where we're at on the calendar map, we'll go on with this journey that isn't really getting any shorter because it's already taken this long to get here, which is a place where we are almost starting over again. It's cause to wonder what's so important about a woman's lone shoe lying in a Honolulu intersection, and one man's few months wandering back and forth, up and down, over and across America with a brief touching of Canada.

Hopefully, something more exciting will happen soon.

That would be nice.

Maybe this will be a start: I don't want to know which room she hanged herself in. One day somebody who knew started to tell and I said I didn't want to know. They were nice enough not to go on with it any further. The subject was left there, unfinished at the kitchen table in the house.

We were eating dinner at the time and also I didn't want her suicide to be part of the dinner. I can't remember what we had for dinner, but there was no way that the death of an unfortunate woman would add an enhancing spice to what we were eating.

When one goes to the spice section of a market and looks among oregano, sweet basil, coriander seeds, dill, garlic powder, one does not want to come across death-by-hanging printed on the label of a spice bottle containing ingredients of horrible consequence and description guaranteed to ruin every meal.

You do not want to add death-by-hanging to any recipe you are cooking or if you are having dinner at somebody's house and they serve a dish that has a unique taste to it and you ask the host and cook what that taste is and they announce casually, "Oh, that's a new spice I'm trying out. Do you like it?"

"It's different. I can't place it. What's the name?"

"Death-by-hanging."

I guess now that I'm telling about the woman killing herself we've more or less started this book in a way that is probably more acceptable than pondering the circumstance of a shoe lying in a Honolulu intersection, so I feel a sense and ability of freedom to wander around in the calendar map of physical goings-on described loosely in the 4th, 5th, and 6th paragraphs of this journey.

Today is my birthday.

I sort of remember parties and the presence of loved ones and friends in the past, but none of this will happen today. I am very distant, almost in exile from my own sentimentality. Besides, I couldn't do anything about it, anyway. I just know that I won't be 46 again.

Even if I were a drunk and a singing Irishman on St. Patrick's Day, wearing so much green that I could cover the entire of Australia like a billiard table, it would not favorably affect anyone.

It would not have made sense for me to have told my fellow passengers on the morning train from Berkeley to San Francisco, none of whom I had ever seen before or would probably ever see again, that it was my birthday.

If I had turned to the complete stranger sitting next to me as we traveled in the tunnel under San Francisco Bay, with fish swimming in the water above us, and said, "Today is my birthday. I'm 47," it would have made everybody feel very uncomfortable.

First, they would have pretended that I was talking to myself. It's a lot easier to imagine that people are talking to themselves, rather than talking directly to you. When people are talking directly to you, it takes an added and more uncomfortable effort to ignore them.

What if I had been more persistent and insisted that people know about this so-called personal holiday of myself, i.e., my birthday, and repeated, "Today is my birthday. I'm 47," in a manner to show unmistakably that I was not talking to myself but was addressing my fellow strangers?

It would have made things worse and filled people with an ominous dread.

What was I going to do next?

I had already said, "Today is my birthday. I'm 47," and then repeated it to everybody's uncomfortable and growing dissatisfaction. They all knew now that I was capable of anything.

Would I reveal 20 sticks of dynamite strapped to my body and hijack the train, demanding that we all be taken to my birthday planet Uranus, legendary sanctuary and powerhouse of Aquarius?

Some of the passengers would be riding on the edge of panic. They could see themselves as a newspaper headline: TRAIN HELD HOSTAGE BY MAN CELEBRATING BIRTH-DAY.

Others would just want to get to where they were going on time. There are always the practical among us. They sort out the priorities and expect nothing more.

I of course said nothing on the train. I was a good passenger. I kept my mouth shut and got off at my appointed station. I just know that I won't be 46 again.

January 30, 1982 Continuing . . .

- 5 -

My trip to Canada in October was wasted. At that time in my life I probably should have gone to any other place in the world but Canada. It was just a whim of fancy that took me there. I'm basically a very poor traveler. It's kind of strange that I do so much traveling for somebody who isn't very good at it.

To begin with: I don't even know how to pack. I'm always packing too many of the wrong things and not enough of the right things. I guess even that would be OK, tolerable, but I worry constantly about it and often think about the logistics of my packing long after the trip is over.

I'm still thinking about a trip that I took to Colorado in 1980 when I packed six pairs of pants and only two shirts. What in the hell was I going to do with six pairs of pants on a two-week trip to Colorado? I needed more shirts. It should have been the other way around. I should have packed six shirts and two pairs of pants. That would have made a hell-of-a-lot more sense, because the weather was so hot in Colorado grasshoppers were eating people's gardens right out from underneath their salads, and I only had two shirts.

Women used to pack for me when I traveled, and always did a good job. No woman ever packed six pairs of pants and only two shirts, but women are too expensive for me now, and I can't afford another one packing my suitcase for a very, very long time.

I think if I were to watch a woman packing a suitcase for

me now, it would be like watching the meter running on a taxicab taking me to a longer distance than I had anticipated and anxiously beginning to wonder if I have enough to pay the fare.

Toronto will always be like the flipside of a dream for me.

I called heads but Toronto came up tails.

One Sunday afternoon I took the streetcar to see some Chinese movies in a district that was outside of Toronto's Chinatown.

I had never been to a Chinese movie theater that wasn't in Chinatown before. Whenever I go to any city that has a Chinatown, I visit it. In the winter of 1980 I spent a week in Vancouver, British Columbia, but from what I could see there, all the Chinese movie theaters were in Chinatown, but not so in Toronto, and I found myself on a streetcar, carrying in my mind directions from a now forgotten origin, riding toward a misplaced Chinese movie theater in Canada. It would have been easier if the theater had been in Chinatown. It's a logical location.

When I got to the theater, it was showing two American motion pictures. One does not normally go to a Chinese movie theater to see American movies. Also, would it be out of line to think that a Chinese movie theater should show Chinese movies?

Coming attraction posters indicated that some Chinese movies would be shown in the following weeks. I couldn't wait, which was probably a good decision, because next week I was back in San Francisco. The Chinese movies coming to Canada next week would never have done me any good.

What else did I do in Toronto?

I had a very bitter affair with a Canadian woman, who was really a nice person. It ended abruptly and badly, which was totally my fault. It would be convenient if one could redesign the past, change a few things here and there, like certain acts of outrageous stupidity, but if one could do that, the past would always be in motion. It would never settle down finally to days of solid marble.

I remember waking up with her that first morning after I spent the night at her apartment and she said, "It's a beautiful day here in Toronto and you're with a nice Canadian girl."

It was.

She was.

January 30, 1982 Finished.

I don't know why I wanted a photograph of me and a chicken in Hawaii. Obsessions are curious things, and they can't help but make a person wonder.

It rained on and off the morning the photograph was taken. There had been a storm the night before, and it was still continuing to rain the following morning. Frankly, I didn't think the weather conditions would permit a photograph to be taken, but the person who took the photograph was optimistic. They had also located the chicken.

I don't know how easy it is to find a chicken in Hawaii, but I was impressed. I am of course not talking about a chicken that is wearing an outfit suitable for a frying pan.

I'm talking about a living chicken, feathers and all.

The photographer called up on the telephone.

"Let's try it," he said.

"Trying it" meaning the actualization of one man's fantasy.

What had concerned us was getting caught in a monsoon-like downpour that would also affect available light, because the photograph had to be taken outside to show the presence of Hawaii.

There would be no reason for the photograph of me and a chicken if Hawaii was not a character in the picture. I wanted to have the picture framed and hanging on the wall of my ranch in Montana.

People would visit me there and maybe one of them would ask about the curious photograph of me and a chicken, hanging interrogatively on the wall. Perhaps they would sense there was a story behind the photograph. It would be fascinating to see how they would verbalize their curiosity. Maybe they would say, "Interesting photograph," and if they got no response: "Where was it taken?"

"Hawaii."

"Is that a chicken?"

"Yes."

"Is there a reason for that photograph? Is that some kind of special chicken?"

Now I would see how determined or not determined they were.

"No, I just wanted to have a photograph of me and a chicken taken in Hawaii."

Where in the hell could they go from there? Where could you and I go from there if we were suddenly placed in that position? I haven't the slightest idea what I would do. I'd probably change the subject or go into another room. I don't think it would be a very good idea to fall helplessly into silence and just stand there staring at a photograph of somebody and a chicken taken together in Hawaii, waiting to be put out of my misery.

Of course it's a retreat, but it beats still standing sort of dumbfounded in the front room, staring at the photograph of an idiot holding a chicken in Hawaii.

It was beautiful back in the mountains behind Honolulu, lush and provocative like an airplane ad flying you to a well-documented and predictable paradise.

There were a lot of chickens running free to choose from and soon I was holding one of them in my hands and the photographer was snapping away. We were worried that there wouldn't be enough light, but it turned out that the light was no problem.

The chicken was very quiet in my hands, probably wondering what was going on. Having its picture taken definitely wasn't part of this chicken's everyday routine. Not many tourists want to have photographs taken of themselves holding chickens in Hawaii.

The chicken was very quiet and serious in my hands. Oh, God, that chicken was serious! After the photograph was taken, I put the chicken down. It walked slowly and bewilderedly away, feathers downcast.

Last week after I got off the train in Berkeley and walked home to the house where the woman had hanged herself, I saw a cat walking across the street in front of me.

Having nothing better to do and being a mammal myself, I said hello to the cat. "Hi, kitty," I said, and then to really put the greeting across, I added, "Meow."

The cat that was hurrying across the street slowed down at the sound of my greeting and then continued slowing down, coming to just standing there looking at me.

I said, "Meow," again with the cat looking at me.

I passed out of the cat's sight as I walked around the corner and started up the hill toward the house where the woman had hanged herself about a year ago.

After she hanged herself, her husband left everything just the way it was the day she committed suicide, and still very little of it had been changed. 1980s Christmas cards were still on the mantel, but the thing that really got me was the kitchen and I will go into it in detail later on. The dead woman's kitchen demands its own time and attention and this is not that time.

As I walked up the hill toward the house, I was thinking about the cat that I had said hello "meow" to and cats in general and my intelligence soon found a single focus.

Cats don't know that people are writing books about them that are splashed all over the best-seller lists and that millions of people are laughing at books filled with cat cartoons.

If you were to show a book full of cat cartoons to a cat: Frankly, it wouldn't give a damn.

February 1, 1982 Finished.

I tossed the bottle of tequila across the street in Ketchikan and the young Alaskan state legislator caught it without hesitation, effortlessly, maybe because he liked to drink tequila.

It was a wonderful drunken night in Alaska.

Before I launched the bottle toward him, I said, "Here, catch, wild legislator." That's what I had taken to calling him, though we had just met that evening.

A group of us funnying and laughing wandered through the streets of Ketchikan, one of the most beautiful towns I have ever visited.

Ketchikan flows like a dream of wooden houses and buildings around the base of Deer Mountain, whose heavily wooded slopes come right down to the town, beautifully nudging it with spruce trees.

The population of Ketchikan, 7,000, and the integrity of the town is virtually unspoiled by a form of style and architecture that could be described as "Los Angeles."

There is no endless street of franchise restaurants and automobile-oriented business. There are no shopping malls to flagrantly disrupt the simplicity of commerce. When people want to buy something, they can just walk down to the store.

So much of America, even what were once unspoilable beautiful towns, look as if "Los Angeles" had overflowed on them like a toilet bowl whose defecated contents all have something to do with the lifestyle of the automobile.

I think the worst case of "Los Angeles" automobile cultural damage I've ever seen is Honolulu. For all practical purposes of survival you might as well drop dead if you don't have a car in Honolulu.

I'm not talking about being a tourist at Waikiki and lying around like a suntan lotion postage stamp on the beach, mounted right next to thousands of other postage stamps in a stamp collector's album owned and operated by the sun.

I'm referring to living in Honolulu.

I think I saw more cars there than I ever saw people.

Often whenever I saw somebody just walking down the street with their feet actually touching the ground and not accompanied by four wheels and a metal eggshell around them, I was startled.

I almost felt like stopping the car I was driving in and offering the person sympathy for the circumstances of misfortune that had led them to walking.

A folksinger has written a song about Honolulu in which she mentions tearing down paradise and putting up a parking lot.

I saw a downtown restaurant that had a sidewalk café as a part of the restaurant. It was a rainy day and nobody was sitting there. "That must be an interesting place to sit and watch people when the weather's good," I said to the woman I was, of course, driving with, because it really doesn't make any sense to try and walk around Honolulu. It's a problem of you can't get there from here that would have baffled Einstein. $E=MC^2$ was duck soup compared to Honolulu traffic.

"You used the wrong word," she said.

"What do you mean?" I said.

"Cars. You watch cars, not people."

We drove on to the next place where we had to drive because if we didn't drive there, we wouldn't be able to find a parking space, and that's very important in Honolulu. I think that I would find automobiles a little more interesting if they carried their own parking space with them.

When I arrived in Honolulu from Alaska, I saw a bird flying around in the Honolulu International Airport. I had never seen a bird inside an airport before. It flew casually around people boarding airplanes, and people just getting off them.

The bird did not act frightened as if it had accidentally been trapped in the airport. The bird was quite comfortable. I think the airport was its home and this was a poetic life, not touched by fear of flying. Also, the bird was perhaps an omen, a portent of the chicken photograph.

When I stepped outside the airport, a Japanese woman was waiting for me, and I got into her car, not knowing what I was really getting into, which became a way of life when Los

Angeles visited Hawaii on vacation but decided not to go home.

Oh, yes, I forgot to mention there's been a change in the calendar map. I moved out of Berkeley yesterday and came back across to stay in San Francisco for two weeks before I go to Chicago.

What led me to leave the house where the woman hanged herself needs a few days sorting through details before I perhaps attempt to describe my leaving or I may not put it down at all. I probably should because in a remote way it has something to do with the woman hanging herself.

But, also, we must not forget that this is the route of a calendar map following one man's existence during a few months' period in time, and I think that it would probably be unfair to ask for perfection if there is such a thing. Probably the closest things to perfection are the huge absolutely empty holes that astronomers have recently discovered in space.

If there's nothing there, how can anything go wrong?

February 1, 1982 Finished.

Speaking of things going not according to plan, the morning that I moved over from the strange house in Berkeley back to San Francisco, the bus taking me here to the Japanese section of town, where I am at a hotel, was rerouted because a building was burning down.

Then the driver stopped and asked us all to get off the bus and change to another bus, so obligingly we all got off, but then somebody came running up to the bus, carrying himself in an official manner and uniform, yelling at the driver, trying to get his attention.

I paid no other attention to what was going on with the bus because I was too busy watching the building burn down. It was a huge fire with smoke rising like a vaporous tower from a disorganized fairy tale that I had failed to finish reading when I was a child or so the smoke seemed.

I had walked away from the other passengers to observe this burning phenomenon of architecture gone awry. It was a huge building and flames were pouring out the roof.

Suddenly, almost instinctively, I turned around and saw the bus I had just gotten off driving away with all the passengers back on it. We all got off when we were told to, and then they all got back on again, except of course for me. I think it had something to do with the official who was running up to the bus, yelling. He must have told the driver to let the passengers return to the bus, which they all did, except for one passenger who was busy watching the fire.

That passenger decided to walk to his hotel.

He did not want to deal anymore that morning with buses that had revolving doors. The fire was on the way to his hotel, so he stopped briefly and watched the flamey doings. The passenger had never been fascinated with burning buildings before, so his watching the fire was an exception to his lifestyle.

There were three ladder trucks with firemen on top of long-flame-reaching ladders pouring water down on the fire, and there was a good crowd of people watching the building go.

The passenger noticed that there was almost a festive feeling among the observers. Many were smiling and some of them were laughing. Not attending fires regularly, preferring movies, he was fascinated by this.

A man complete with a sleeping bag and backpack containing what he called his life was sitting down across the street from the fire drinking a bottle of wino-type wine. The man looked as if wherever he went was his address, and only a bloodhound had any possibility of delivering his mail.

He enjoyed long, carefully thought-out sips of wine from a bottle in a paper bag while he watched the building burn down. It would be an easy matter for a trained mail-delivering bloodhound to track this man down. All the dog would have to do would be to follow a trail of paper bags with empty wine bottles in them to deliver this man a letter from his mother saying: "Don't ever come home again and stop calling. We don't want to have anything to do with you anymore. Get a job. —Love, your ex-mother."

It was not a building occupied on a Sunday morning, so there was no drama of life and death to mar or perhaps enhance the fire viewing. The passenger had no idea why people gathered to watch buildings burn down, especially if it had nothing to do with them, if it wasn't their house burning down or one nearby threatening to burn down where they lived.

Yes, the passenger found it all very different and interesting, and then he remembered a woman that he had been involved with years ago. They'd had an often very intense love affair that occupied large portions of his time in the late 1960s and finally dwindled out in the early 1970s. It was the kind of involvement referred to as "off and on."

During a time when he was not seeing her, she had picked up an undue interest in fires and become a firetruck chaser. She would go out of her way anytime, day or night, to be at the site of a burning building. One morning around 4 a.m., she found herself watching a duplex join the kingdom of ashes and ruin when she noticed that she was wearing a bathrobe over her pajamas and had a pair of slippers on. She had just jumped out of bed when she heard the sound of nearby fire engines, slipped on her bathrobe, put on her slippers, and headed out the door toward the fire.

She had been watching the fire for about half an hour before she noticed what she was wearing. Her attire startled her. She had gone a little too far, so she hung fire-watching up.

She had absolutely no interest in becoming a nut.

She probably wondered how it had gotten this far.

She went home and vowed to denounce the siren call of sirens.

The passenger years later, watching a building burn down in San Francisco, decided spontaneously to call her on the telephone if she still lived in San Francisco. She had done a lot of traveling since he had known her in the later 60s. The last time he had seen her, accidentally meeting, she was living in San Francisco.

Perhaps she was still there.

He decided to call her up from a telephone booth right across the street from the fire. It seemed like a logical thing to do for a passenger whose bus had gone off without him.

What are old former fire-groupie lovers for?

The passenger dialed information and sure enough, she still lived in town. He called her and when she answered, she immediately identified the passenger's voice, though he had only said, "Hello," and she said hello back using his given name, which of course was not Passenger.

Though it would have been slightly amusing if she had said, "Hello, Passenger."

That would have startled and given the passenger cause to think.

But no such thing happened, thank God, and the passenger returned her greeting by saying, "I was just thinking about you."

"Oh," she said.

"Yes," he said. "I'm watching a building burn down, and I thought I'd give you a call."

She laughed.

"I'm right across the street from it," he said.

She laughed again and said, "I just heard about it on the radio. They say the smoke is eight stories high."

"Yeah," the passenger said. "And there are three firemen

standing at the end of ladders pouring water down onto the roof, but you probably know more about this than I do."

Again: laughter.

"Well," the passenger said. "That's about it. The next time I see something burning down, I'll give you a call."

"You do that," she said.

They both pleasantly hung up.

In the past there had been many exchanges between them that were not nearly as pleasant. The passenger thought about their past together: of first meeting, then becoming lovers, and days and nights together, crossing from one decade into another and then events crumbling away into blank years and the silence of emotional ruins.

The passenger thought about the telephone call that he had just made to her. Somehow it seemed perfect in its bizarre logic.

He never would have made that telephone call if the bus had not driven off without him, stranding him at the site of the fire, which he decided to investigate, having nothing better to do, and being on the calendar map that February Sunday morning of his strange wanderings, which started out innocently enough when he left Montana in late September.

I guess that's what a passenger's supposed to do, pass from one place to another, but it doesn't make it any simpler. About all you can do is wish him luck, and hope that he has some slight understanding of what uncontrollably is happening to him.

Why am I suddenly back in Alaska being driven down a

road by somebody who is insisting on taking me somewhere to look at fake totem poles? I guess this is just the way it happens if you have lost control of days, weeks, months, and years.

I've seen real ones in the museum of anthropology at the University of British Columbia, but I humor the man who wants to take me to see fake totem poles in Ketchikan, Alaska, because he is a nice man and wants to be a good host, guide, and some fake totem poles are part of his itinerary for me.

As we drive toward the fake totem poles, he tells me about his love life, which in no way did I encourage him to get started on. He has a very complicated love life and I think he wants some good useful advice from me to maybe help sort out and make sense of it.

But I just feel uncomfortable driving along toward some fake totem poles in Alaska. After that night when people asked me what I did that afternoon and I told them, they all said, "Why did he take you out there? Those are fake totem poles," and I have no answer for them as I had none for the man's love life.

I could not afford the luxury of a complicated love life. I had a simple love life and often when I have a simple love life, I don't have any love life at all. I sort of miss it, but the complications all return soon enough, and I find myself occupying sleepless nights, wondering how I lost control of the heart's basic events again.

We had to walk through some woods to get to the fake totem poles.

The man didn't talk about his love life in the woods. Instead he gave the local names of the vegetation that we walked through to get to the fake totem poles. As we walked along, it was as if he were reading from a living list, which I would forget as fast as he would check it off.

After a while I wished that he would go back to talking about his love life. At least then I wouldn't feel guilty if I should forget something.

I've never really been very interested in remembering things that did not immediately catch my attention. I think this is a character weakness, but it's a little late to do anything about it now.

I've just turned 47 and I can't go back into the past and realign my priorities in such a way as to create another personality out of them. I'm just going to have to make do with the almost five decades sum of me.

It may not add up to the total I had envisioned for myself when I was younger and not as warped as I am now, but I just can't copy a list of plants down that I saw briefly in my mind on the way to some fake totem poles.

The totem poles were very, very fake.

When we drove back to Ketchikan, it started raining. A cold bleak December rain fell out of the sky, and the man went back to talking about his love life, and I felt as if I were slowly shrinking in the car, getting smaller, almost childlike.

The windshield wipers kept even with the rain, but the man's endless and complicated love life was a losing battle for me. As we drove back into Ketchikan, my feet were no longer touching the floor and my clothes hung about me like a tent.

That man's love life really made a mess out of me on a rainy afternoon in Alaska. I wish I could have said something that would have been helpful to him, but I didn't feel qualified after the shoes fell off my feet onto the floor of the car.

The man graciously pretended not to notice.

The second after he stopped talking about his love life and it was certain that he wasn't going to bring it up again, I returned instantly back to normal size, which was naturally quite a relief to me.

Somehow my shoes were back on my feet and I could walk with them toward other things.

One of those things being a Japanese cemetery on the island of Maui in Hawaii, but first there will be an abrupt digression here because somehow I feel if I don't write the following, it will never get written, so please have patience with me and I'll get back to the Japanese cemetery in Hawaii as soon as possible.

The thing that has caused me to briefly interrupt the Japanese cemetery is something that I read in a Japanese novel a few years ago about a man meeting a woman in a supermarket in Tokyo who became the lover of the narrator. I think it would be so exotic to meet a future lover for the first time in a supermarket.

I've thought about this a lot, especially recently with what little grocery shopping I did in Berkeley when I was staying at the house where the woman hanged herself.

I would go shopping at the nearby supermarket, pushing my cart around, buying random food that I really had no interest in eating, other than daily demanded nutritional need.

. . . and sometimes I would think about the Japanese novel and meeting a new lover while shopping at a supermarket. How unique and bizarre a place for a chance, intimate meeting!

February 3, 1982 Finished.

I wonder how this supermarket love affair would begin and who would first initiate it. Would I be standing in the soup section going over the possibilities offered? Perhaps a can of tomato soup might be nice on a rainy day when suddenly a blond woman's voice would interrupt my brief meditation.

I didn't even hear her approaching. I don't think she snuck up on me with her shopping cart. It's just that I wasn't paying attention or maybe she did sneak up on me, stalking me in the soup section.

"Hello," she said, her voice pleasantly inviting.

I would look startled away from a shelf where tomato soup was being displayed for a possible rainy day's lunch.

I used to go out with blondes.

Actually, I once had a thing for them.

The sight of the blond woman made me happy. I wonder why I wasn't aware of her approach. She followed her hello with an "Excuse me, but haven't we met before?"

I actually had a woman say that to me at a party, which led to a brief one-nocturnal stand.

But this was a different woman.

Who knows how it would end?

We got in line together at the checkout stand because she had offered me a ride home, but first of course I would have a drink at her place, seeing that it was on the way home, home being a place where another woman had hanged herself.

The shopper in front of us at the checkout stand had 5,000 things in her train of shopping carts, which gave us some time to get to know each other.

Her name was X and she had recently graduated from the University of California at Berkeley, where she had majored in philosophy, but she couldn't find any jobs that wanted a person who knew lots about philosophy, so she was working temporarily at a boutique in Walnut Creek, and, no, she did not make it a habit to talk to strange men in supermarkets, but there was something about the way I was staring at the cans of soup that got her attention and on a sudden lark, she wanted to know more about a man who took soup so seriously.

I told her that I was thinking that perhaps I wanted to get a can of tomato soup for a rainy day.

"I figured it had to be something like that," she said.

The woman in front of us was down to 2,399 things as she was emptying the Southern Pacific Railroad of her carts, and the tape unwinding at great length from the cash register was beginning to form itself into a Möbius strip.

"I have a question about the tomato soup," X said. "And please don't take this wrong, but it's not raining now and it hasn't rained in days and the weather prediction is for more of the same."

"It will rain someday," I said.

"I guess it really doesn't make that much difference because you didn't get the tomato soup, anyway," she said.

"Sometimes I think about things before I actually get them," I said. "And that includes soup."

"I'm glad I said hello to you," she said. "I don't meet people like you very often."

Then there was a silent period of watching the woman's carts in front of us being further depleted. The number of things in the carts was now less than a thousand.

The checker had added up so many things from those carts that she acted as if she were helpless in a dream, taking out a can of tuna fish, a box of rice, a cube of butter, a package of napkins, a box of plastic spoons, a carton of detergent, a dog collar, a jar of mustard, one banana, a bottle of vinegar, and so forth, etc.

As the stuff was being added up, a young man was bagging it. He was working on his 50th bag. His face had the starkness of an inmate on Devil's Island.

If he was working his way through college, he had been a freshman when he started bagging this stuff and now he was a senior.

X smiled at me. It was a smile that communicated that we would soon be out of there and enjoying ourselves at her place, sipping glasses of white wine and learning more about each other.

Perhaps we would make some jokes about all the groceries the shopper in front of us had packed into her carts or we would talk about things that were intimate that would lead us more quickly into arriving at her bed.

But something was going to have to happen very quickly in that soup section because I couldn't stand there forever staring at cans of tomato soup.

She was going to have to come along very soon and get this love affair started before the store closed or I would only go on thinking about that haunting Japanese novel and never be a romantic participant in a supermarket love affair and instead be in Hawaii, wandering about a Japanese cemetery with the Pacific Ocean acting out one of its boundaries.

The cemetery is run down and a Japanese elderly couple are futilely trying to make it look better. They are not happy with the sloppy condition of the cemetery and complain about its disrepair, but there is obviously too much work for them to do to make the cemetery live up to their standards of how it should look.

It is around noon and the heat is oppressing and the sun shines down lacking any quality of mercy.

I am in the company of the Japanese woman who picked me up at the airport in Honolulu. She humored me when I pointed out the cemetery and asked that we stop to look at it.

She knows that my ways and interests are often strange, and she humors me because I'm not always weird, just some of the time. Often, I can be stultifyingly boring, which has been pointed out more than once. I mean, I can go for weeks at a time living like a denizen at the bottom of a terrarium.

I can be almost helpless in my lack of interest and activity, but this is not the case today in this Japanese cemetery on the island of Maui here in Hawaii.

Most people when they come to Hawaii do not come for the cemeteries. They are interested in the sun and the beaches: two things that I've never really cared for, so I'm kind of displaced here in Hawaii, but I make do with what I have, and what I have right now is this Japanese cemetery to explore.

There is a Buddhist shrine beside the cemetery.

The Japanese woman, who was born and raised on Maui, tells me that she has relatives buried in this cemetery and she attended their funerals. I don't ask who and where they are among the dead. The Japanese woman and I go our own separate ways. I just stroll about creating my own trails above these signatures of immortality, and I lose track of her.

I've always been fascinated by cemeteries and have probably spent too much time of my limited living time in hundreds of them wherever I've been in this world.

Once I was very sick staying in a small cabin back in the woods of Mendocino. I had been working without a vacation for two years, and then a girlfriend insisted that I stop work, take some time off, and go with her for a few weeks to a cabin up the coast of California near the little gothic town of Mendocino. Somebody had loaned her the cabin and she had borrowed somebody else's car for two weeks to take us there.

She really wanted me to take a vacation, and so she had arranged everything. The day after we arrived there, I got sick and was sick until the day we left.

It was really not the vacation that she had counted on.

I had a high fever that alternated with bone-rattling chills, and the days passed like years lying in bed. There was a huge picture window just a few feet away from the end of the bed, and I would stare out the window at the forest that came almost up to the window.

The forest was dense second-growth timber, and there was no other perspective than the trees, which were often very dark in their greenness because not only was a I very sick but the weather matched my illness with low overcast clouds, and low hanging fogs and mists like coat hangers for the clothes of the dead.

It was a hell-of-a place to put a huge picture window just staring at an overwhelming closeness of trees. There was no space in between them. They were absolute. The person whose house it was must have really liked to look at trees because that's all there was to look at out that window.

So I just lay there sweating and shaking and looking at all those goddamn trees.

The woman who brought me there had not planned on

spending all of her time with a sick person, so she went out often to visit friends, and walk around the town, and do things with her friends: dinners and parties, etc.

I was so sick that I couldn't do anything.

Once because I knew the woman was very bored, I summoned up all the remaining energy that I had and tried to make love to her, but my body failed me.

Afterwards we lay there in bed and she told me that she hadn't thought that it was a very good idea in the first place, which she had told me but I had insisted that I could make love, alas, my body proved me wrong.

The woman got out of bed and dressed.

It had also been a frustrating experience for her.

She went out to have a cup of coffee with a woman dancer that she was friends with in town, and I guess talk about dancing, which she was very curious about.

There was a sort of interesting thing about the dancer. I had met her in San Francisco three or four years before and was quite smitten by her. She was about 20, then, but looked innocently 15 and dancing in a ballet that I saw a number of times in rehearsal and performance.

She had a very, very interesting body with breasts that were a little too large for a ballet dancer. She was also blond and very next-door-neighbor cute. She unfortunately had a very lackadaisical approach to dancing which I think eventually led her to give it up.

Once during rehearsal there was a scene in the ballet where

she was to lie motionless on the floor, wearing a black leotard. The other dancers would dance around her and then after five stationary minutes, she would get up and start dancing with them again.

The five minutes passed in which she did not move at all, just lay there rather invitingly on the floor. When it was her turn to return to the motion of the ballet, she continued not moving. It was important for her to join the ballet now, but she continued lying there.

"Hey, S," one of the dancers said and then finally yelled, "S!" to no avail. She was asleep. The other dancers had to stop the ballet and wake her up.

She looked confused and had a sleepy just-waking-up eroticism to her.

I think she quit the group shortly after that and I did not see her again until last week in Mendocino.

There was a break in my sickness and the weather. It was actually sunny for a few hours and the flu went into a dull remission. My girlfriend and I went and met the dancer and a male friend at a beach on a little river.

I guess we had a sort of cliché French bread, cheese, Greek olives, and white wine picnic. Maybe a little fruit, too. It was actually warm there at the beach. Both of the women were wearing two-piece bathing suits. The dancer was wearing a bikini and my friend was wearing a more conservative suit.

Suddenly, without much, I should say *any*, ado, they took their tops off and there I was looking at the dancer's breasts, which were too large for a dancer. She still looked 20 (15) and we continued on with the picnic as if it were perfectly normal paying no obvious attention, for the two women to have their breasts exposed.

Anyway, my girlfriend's having coffee with the dancer was far more rewarding than trying to make love with a sick person. After she left, I went back to staring out the window at the trees. Suddenly I just couldn't take them anymore. I struggled out of bed and into my clothes. I had a fever, but I didn't care. There was an old bicycle leaning up against the house. It was a girl's bicycle and I pedaled very slowly, just short of falling over, down to a cemetery near the town. It was maybe a half-a-mile journey but seemed like a continent to me.

I got off the bicycle and walked among the tombstones, studying their messages of death. It was an old California cemetery. Many of the dead had been there for a long time.

The sky was very overcast and so low that it had become almost a drizzle.

I was burning up with fever as I wandered around reading the dead, but somehow it made me feel more alive than just staring at trees before, during, and after failing at love.

I got back on the bicycle and pedaled barely faster than a statue of somebody pedaling a bicycle slowly to the bed and staring out the window at the trees again.

When my girlfriend came back, she tried to be cheerful and brought me a glass of orange juice and sat down on the edge of the bed and said that I would get better soon. She was right, and now eighteen years later, I was on an island thousands of miles away from that window in the California woods, and my seemingly endless forested sickness, and I was among these Japanese graves which held my attention, and the sound of the neighboring ocean is the music of their silence.

February 4, 1982 Continuing . . .

I notice something interesting, different, in this cemetery. It appears to be a pile of tombstones stacked together around the base of what seems to be a monument at the ocean's edge. I go over to it, walking along a row of poles strung with decayed electric wire.

Once upon a time the wire brought light to the end of the cemetery, but the system has been allowed to deteriorate, so now it is capable only of darkness.

Nobody wants to have lights on anymore in the cemetery.

They have decided that there is no reason for the cemetery to be lit at night.

There is a strange melancholy to the decayed electric wire.

I wonder if it remembers when it served a purpose: lighting the dead and casting their shadows upon the never-ending motion and gestures of the sea.

Then I am standing beside the pile of tombstones.

There are hundreds of them here.

I can't figure out why.

Are they a part of some ceremony that has to deal with the monument they are piled randomly around? It is a mystery that I have to find the answer to.

February 4, 1982 Finished.

I wander away from the pile of tombstones and go over to the Japanese woman and ask her about it. She has no idea either and looks over at the elderly Japanese couple fussing anonymously with the impossible task of returning the cemetery to a previous order that they once knew.

Maybe this was a very neat cemetery back in the 1930s, and that's the cemetery they remember and want it to be again.

"I'll ask them," she says, being very patient and helpful with my strange pastime. She likes to sunbathe on the beach and swim in the ocean. I am probably the only tourist she has ever had visit her whose interest was in cemeteries instead of the beautiful beaches of Hawaii.

She goes over and talks to them. The couple talks to her for a few moments and seem to be very upset and often gesture at the cemetery. The old woman makes short gestures and the man makes wide, sweeping gestures. His gestures often encompass the entire cemetery, leaving out not a single tombstone.

The Japanese woman comes back.

"They are very unhappy with the condition of this cemetery," she says.

"I know," I say.

"They say that nobody cares anymore and they can't do it all by themselves. They wonder what's happening to the world."

"What about the pile of tombstones?"

"Oh, them," the Japanese woman says. She has been thinking seriously about what the old couple had been telling her.

"They say those tombstones are from graves that were dug up because the families didn't want the responsibility of keeping them up anymore."

"What about the bodies?" I ask, looking over at the pile of tombstones by the ocean's edge. "What did they do with the bodies?"

"If they needed to be cremated, they were cremated and then put with the ashes of other people in the shrine," she said.

I looked over at the Buddhist shrine.

It was tired and worn out in the sun.

"They keep the ashes in there," she said, glancing at the shrine.

I looked back at the pile of tombstones.

"I wonder why they put the tombstones over there."

"I guess they don't want to throw them away," she said.

"It's sad," I said. "Now nobody knows they even lived."

A lot of the tombstones were piled in such a way that you couldn't see whose lives they represented. You could only see the backs of the tombstones. The person's name and birth date and death date were hidden from view.

It was as if they had never existed.

I looked over at the shrine.

It was such an anonymous place to be interred, and the paint was falling off.

A person couldn't just drive by one day as I had just done and get out of the car and walk among the dead, thinking about them, wondering who they were and how they had lived.

Being in the shrine, they were out of sight and out of mind. I had a feeling that the relatives who'd had them dug up and then put in the shrine did not visit their memories very often.

It was the way the tombstones were randomly abandoned that offered help to that conclusion. I walked back to the pile of tombstones to have a final viewing of them. I knew their story and could not help but feel bad, knowing that their friends and relatives had moved away from their death, not wanting to keep it up, anymore.

I thought it was so strange.

Why not leave them in the ground where they had been put in the first place accompanied by a funeral of respect and mourning? It was not that the cemetery had a shortage of spaces. If the dead were going to be interred in the shrine, that should have been done in the first place.

This pile of forgotten tombstones made no sense at all to me. I guess it is a part of everything else, including this.

I turned and walked back to the other side of the cemetery where the Japanese woman was waiting. She was tired of the cemetery and wanted to go. We had to fly back to Honolulu in a few hours and were supposed to have lunch at a restaurant that her mother owned before we left.

I walked past the old couple struggling with the disrepair of the cemetery.

They looked up, but didn't say anything.

"I guess we should leave," I said.

"Yes," the Japanese woman said. "We don't have much time. We should catch the two-o'clock airplane, so I can take a little nap at home before I go to work this evening. We'll drive directly to the restaurant for lunch."

She already had a busy itinerary for the living to follow.

Whereas my itinerary was still with the dead who are just moved around helplessly from one place to another.

We got into the car and drove slowly away.

"My mother makes good tempura," she said.

I was going to turn around and take one last look at the Japanese cemetery before it disappeared completely from sight but then I changed my mind. They would have to get along without me from now on.

I knew that I would never return there again.

The Japanese cemetery was the most interesting thing I

had seen on the island of Maui, and there would be no reason for me to return to Maui. I had used it up. Too bad I'm not a sun lover. It probably would make my life a bit simpler to just lie around in the sun and slowly turn myself over like a thinking barbecue to cook the other side.

Farewell, Maui, island of sunshine.

Farewell, Japanese cemetery, with your dead that move around.

Buffalo, New York, was very nice for the first day.

I had gone there to give a couple of lectures and to visit with an old friend and his wife. They lived in a large cottage on a small quiet lane that reminded me of the Hampstead area in London.

I was looking forward to a pleasant stay in Buffalo. I had been there before and found the architecture to be very charming. Buffalo has a great many huge brick houses built in a time when they could be afforded, a time that will never come again.

There were three cottages on the little lane where my friend lived. I was staying at an old hotel within walking distance. I looked forward to good and renewing times. My energy and spirit were exhausted from a hard summer's work in Montana and a period of intense income tax activity, ending just before I came to Buffalo.

The next morning I called my friend up from the hotel, planning to spend another good day with him and his wife. When he answered the telephone, he sounded tired and distracted. Then he told me that the young woman who lived by herself in the cottage next to theirs had been raped that night.

I walked over to my friend's cottage, where the atmosphere was very slow and formal with shock. We drank some very slow cups of coffee. Two detectives came by. They were thoughtful and serious with their questions and then left.

I knew that my stay in Buffalo was not going to be the one I had planned on because the atmosphere was suddenly darkened by the shadow of the young woman's ordeal.

The next day I called my friend again and this time he answered the telephone in a very shaken way.

The man who had raped the woman had broken into their cottage that night and without making a sound had entered their bedroom to be discovered by his wife, who woke up to find the man wandering around the room.

She had loudly awakened her husband, whose startled entrance into waking helped drive the man from their bedroom and out of the cottage, but not before grabbing my friend's pants on the way out.

For the second morning in a row, I walked with consternation over to my friend's cottage and listened to a story of horror. It was such a quiet little lane and this is what had happened two nights in a row among the possibility of three cottages.

The detectives had already been there and gone.

This time instead of very slow and time-extended cups of coffee, some whiskey was in order.

The man who had broken into the cottage had not stolen

anything except my friend's pants. There were a lot of things that he could have stolen, seeing that he had the run of the cottage except for their bedroom, but he didn't touch any of them. There were tape recorders and stereo stuff, but he didn't want them.

What did he want?

He had spent a considerable time breaking into their cottage, coming in through a heavily secured bathroom window. He had to really work at breaking into the cottage.

My friend was very curious about the dedication of the man, so he went outside to take another look to see if he could find anything more about what had happened, leaving his wife and me sitting there numbly with our whiskey.

He came back a moment later with a very unhappy expression on his face. He had found something. We followed him outside to a place where a butcher knife was lying on the ground. It was one of those butcher knives that you see used so often in horror movies for the entertainment of moviegoers who like to watch people being chopped up into little pieces.

It was far from entertaining lying there on the ground beside my friend's cottage. The knife had not been there the day before when the woman had been raped. The detectives were called and they returned very seriously, barely talking at all, and took the knife away.

My friends decided that they did not want to spend the night in their cottage. They needed a break from what had been going on the last two nights at their "peaceful" little lane that had originally reminded me of pleasant times spent in London.

So they drove me up to Canada and spent the night in Toronto. I had planned on visiting friends in Toronto after my stay in Buffalo, which was cut short by rape, stolen trousers, and a butcher knife. It didn't make much sense to stay on in Buffalo after that because my friends were going to be busy fortifying their house. Driving me up to Toronto gave them an excuse to get a good night's sleep without wondering what was going to happen next.

I journeyed into Canada under a terrible pall and immediately had a bad love affair which was totally the result of my own actions. The woman wanted it to be pleasant, but I wouldn't allow that to happen. I fucked it up.

I checked out of my hotel room in Toronto and had a couple of hours to waste before I went out to the airport to catch a plane, so I went to a movie and saw a version of Tarzan that starred an actress who was famous for taking off her clothes.

I think the only reason they made the movie was to give her an excuse to take her clothes off. I wonder why they chose the subject of Tarzan to do this. The theater charged a low admission and the sparse audience was basically human derelicts idling away their lives as I was also doing.

It was a cold day in Toronto and maybe some of the men, there were no women, had deliberately mesmerized themselves into believing that they were actually going to get inside the movie, which was filmed in the tropics, and become a part of the heat, but it was just as cold inside the theater as it was outside on the street.

The management of the theater had decided that there was

no reason to warm this misbegotten audience of transients, including myself.

But why Tarzan?

By the time the actress took her clothes off, the audience was so cold that it didn't make any difference and some of them were sleeping in their seats or perhaps had frozen to death. Anyway, they were that still, and the sight of naked flesh could not arouse them.

That evening I found myself back in San Francisco again and it was still October, and I had not been out of Montana even a month. My trip East had turned out exactly the opposite of what I had intended. I just wanted to have some fun and maybe a few pleasant memories along the way.

When I left Montana on September 27, 1981, I felt as if a period in my life had come to an end and I was now embarking on the next stage of my life.

I guess you could call it that because for sure something was happening.

February 5, 1982 Finished.

Now it is early February and the plum trees are in the full of blossoming in the Japanese section of San Francisco where I have been staying for a week, studying this brief calendar map of my life. When I started drawing this calendar the purple plum blossoms were just barely edging out of the dark branches of the trees. The blossoms were pinpoints of purple and now they are a stampede of color.

Soon they will start trickling off the branches onto the ground and by the time that I have completed this calendar map before I go to Chicago, the blossoms will be gone and their brief February spring silenced and no longer immortal.

If I were to mention their existence in Chicago, which has been struck by one of the worst winters of the twentieth century, I think I would have to repeat myself and still not be sure of understanding.

"What did you say again about plum blossoms?" somebody might ask me very politely.

"It's not important," I might answer politely, tired now of trying to explain a tiny little spring event in far-off San Francisco, a city that people have trouble understanding, myself included, anyway.

It would probably be best in Chicago not to bring February plum blossoms up. There are a lot of other topics I can talk about without unduly confusing the people of Chicago.

I could tell them about the strangeness of living in a house where a woman had hanged herself.

Yesterday I saw a friend of mine who is now living in that house, which I am thinking about moving back into tomorrow because my money is running low again and I may not be able to afford staying at the hotel here in the Japanese district much longer. I have been going through a period in which my finances are comical, but that's not the point of this journey.

My friend told me that he had gotten two telephone calls asking to speak to the dead woman. Some people don't keep up on current affairs. The woman had been dead for a year.

I didn't ask my friend how he answered them.

I wonder how you would answer that.

> *"I'm sorry but she's dead."*
> *"Dead?"*
> *"Yes, she hanged herself last year."*
> *"Hanged herself?"*
> *"Yes, I think in the living room. There are some huge wooden beams in the ceiling. That would be a good place to do it."*
> *"Excuse me, but is this telephone number •••-••••?" the person asks.*
> *"Yes."*
> *"Does Mrs. O live there?"*
> *"Not any longer."*

Or . . . the telephone ringing again

> *"Hello."*
> *"May I speak to Mrs. O?"*
> *"No, that's quite impossible."*
> *"Impossible?"*
> *"I can assure you it is impossible for her to speak to you."*

"Who is this?"

Or . . . the telephone ringing *again*

"Hello, is Y"—using her first name—"in?"
"No."
"When do you expect her to return?"
"I'm sorry but I guess you haven't heard. She passed away last year."
"Oh, God!" The voice at the other end of the line starting to weep. "It can't be true."
"I'm sorry."
"Oh, God."

Or . . . the telephone ringing

I wonder if the telephone rang just the second after she hanged herself and she was still alive, conscious, but it was now impossible for her to undo her own hanging, and run it in reverse like a motion picture running backwards, and she wasn't hanging by her neck anymore, and whatever she had hanged herself with was back in its original place. Perhaps in a drawer or on a shelf or hanging from a rack, and the telephone started ringing and she walked over and answered it.

"Hello. Oh, how are you? Sure, let's get together tomorrow for coffee. About three would be fine. I'll meet you there. Your husband's girlfriend huh? We'll talk about it tomorrow. That's right. Tomorrow. Friday. OK, good-bye," instead of the telephone ringing slow, slowly, *slowest ever,* and then fading into oblivion and somebody to find your body and cut it down later.

When I was in Ketchikan, I had a long talk one night with the wild Alaska legislator. He is one of those people who in a normal book, unfortunately not this one, would be developed into a memorable character.

A few days ago I was thinking about how much of him should be betrayed in this writing, because he certainly possesses enough possibility for development. He is a very interesting, you could say colorful, man. He would be a juicy role for a character actor in a movie far different from this book.

We talked, or more accurately yet, he listened to me talk about how I looked forward to arriving at a period of grace in my life, and my late forties might be a good place to start. What I meant by grace was a more realistic approach to the process of living to arrive at perhaps some tranquillity and to place a little more distance between the frustrations and agonies in my life, which are so often of my own creation.

It is interesting that I used the word "realistic."

Instead of having just a few miles and sometimes only inches between my problems, why not increase the distance? It would be nice for a change to have 47 miles between one problem and another, and perhaps in that 47 miles a little peace could grow like daffodils between my problems.

I've always liked daffodils.

They are almost my favorite flower.

I got a letter from the wild legislator a few weeks later

when I was in Hawaii. He said that he wished for grace in my life. He remembered that night in Alaska, and wanted the best for me. What a selfish writer I am, using him only as a mirror to reflect my own ego, and no one to play the part and no movie.

I left for Anchorage the day after we talked about grace in Ketchikan. It was the type of conversation that required or perhaps benefited from lots of strong drink, whiskey for me and tequila for him.

I think we drank in a bar until around four in the morning.

Sometimes it was snowing outside, just beyond our words.

When I woke up later in the morning, I had a terrible hangover and knew I had to fly to Anchorage in a few hours, but before I did that I was to give an interview to the local newspaper.

What was I going to talk about?

I got a hot dog and walked over to the dock, which was right across from the hotel.

My mind and body were not having any fun at all.

Halfway through the hot dog, it suddenly became very uninteresting.

There were some blackbirds at the dock and a freighter under Panamanian registry. Anyway, I think they were black-birds or maybe they were crows. It seems to me through the pain and haze of a just-having-awakened-from-a-hard-night's-drinking that they were crows.

But even in a hangover, the ship had the word "Panama" on

it, so I'm going to call the birds crows and please picture crows whenever I use the word "crows."

Forget all about blackbirds.

Suddenly I knew if I took one more bite of hot dog, I would be courting misfortune. Who wants to puke in front of a ship under Panamanian registry anchored on a quiet morning in Alaska with a bunch of crows staring at you or perhaps was it my hot dog they were interested in?

If I had vomited, I think they would have flown away.

Alaska is a very huge place, and they could easily find someplace else to live out their lives. Alaska is so huge that they could have flown away separately and never seen each other again nor actually seen another crow again, except when they came across their own reflections in the water.

I took what was left of the hot dog bun and threw it to the crows.

They all studied it very carefully and for a long time before one of them made a move for it. This was something to do with my hangover before I was interviewed. I stared at the crows and my hot dog bun.

This is not the kind of travel description that one usually reads about Alaska, and besides, where did I get the hot dog, anyway? some of you are asking. A hot dog is just something that one doesn't associate with Alaska: bears, mountains, Eskimos, yes, a hot dog with mustard and relish, no.

I just got it someplace there in town.

It was not a difficult thing to do.

Now: Trying to eat it was another story.

I got bored watching the crows watching the hot dog bun, so I took another look at the ship to make sure that I hadn't read Panama instead of Switzerland.

It was Panama all right, and one of the crows was now holding a hot dog bun in its mouth. I think it was a first for the crow because he didn't know what to do with it. He just stood there looking ridiculous with the hot dog sticking out of his mouth like a tiny rowboat.

The other crows were fascinated, too.

"This is why I am in Alaska," I said to myself. "To watch a crow with a hot dog bun sticking out of its mouth like a rowboat."

I walked over to a nearby parked car, scattering the crows and the hot dog bun now traveling with them, and got a handful of snow off the hood and rubbed it fiercely on my face.

The interview was just a short time away and I had to make sense.

Maybe I would tell the reporter about the crows and my hot dog bun. It would be a good way to break the ice between us, loosen up and put the interview on a casual footing.

And so I did it.

I wonder what he thought.

When I told him about the crows and the hot dog bun, I was very animated and told him the story using perhaps a little too many gestures. God, I had a horrible hangover. Twice, while telling the story, I stood up at the table where were sitting, having just met, and waved my arms enthusiastically in the air.

I wonder what he wrote.

The flight up to Anchorage seemed forever.

In my Top 40 of terrible things to do in my life is flying with a hangover.

The central nervous system is in direct conflict with the speed and noise of the airplane. It's like having a surgeon operating on you while you're still conscious with a scalpel in one of his hands and a textbook in the other, and meanwhile he is repeating over and over again, "I should have studied harder," and just then his mother barges into the operating room wearing her gardening clothes and comes over to me and looks at the hole in my stomach and yells at the doctor, "Why did I waste my money sending you to medical school!" and then gesturing in my direction, "Look at that hole! What are you going to do now? I want to see how you get out of this one!"

She pulls up a stool right in front of the hole in my stomach.

"OK, wise guy," she says to her son. "Where do you go from here?"

February 6, 1982 Finished.

This next sentence finds me living back in the strange house in Berkeley where the woman hanged herself. Actually, I'm sitting here in a front room, and it's nine February days later, the 15th.

What happened?

Well, what happened is that sometimes we have no control over our lives. My plan was to stay a the hotel in the Japanese section and finish this book and then go to Chicago, come back to San Francisco to take care of things, and then on to Denver, spend a few days in Boulder, Colorado, and afterwards fly to Montana to spend the spring.

Did I say that the house is very old and has a high-ceilinged, darkly wooded interior? It is a wooden house in the classic sense of describing a wood house, so the shadows in the house have been here for a long time, shadows to begin with and then decades of shadows added to those shadows, and also gathering, adding to them this day: Monday the 15th of February 1982.

The day after tomorrow, Wednesday, I go to Chicago, but today I'm here returned by the uncertainties and compulsions of life.

Maybe I'll describe what I have been doing since I interrupted or was interrupted writing this book nine days ago because this book is a calendar of one man's journey during a few months in his life.

I wish I had another calendar to aid in accurately arranging this last week but I guess it's not that important, but I would like to know what day I stopped writing. I don't mean the date. I know the date was February 6, but was it a Saturday or a Sunday? That's what I'm not quite certain of, and what day shortly after I stopped writing did I move back here?

Obviously, I'm not very good at this.

I tried it with my fingers, each finger represented a day, but I fouled it up somehow, which is probably impossible to do. I think what threw me off was trying to relate what day I stopped writing with the day that I moved back here. I don't know why it is suddenly so confusing, but it is. I hope this is not a negative reflection on my current decision-making abilities. Am I doing anything right?

I did not plan on coming back to this house in Berkeley: ever. It would no longer be a part of my life. I would do other things, stay someplace else, sleep in different beds.

But it didn't turn out that way.

I decided to come back here for five or six reasons. Only, one of them is interesting. I felt as if I needed more time in the atmosphere of the house. I needed to become more aware of its role in eternity.

So I am back sleeping upstairs in the bed she once slept in, and wandering around all the antiques and objects of this house. It is raining hard outside making an afternoon winterstorm happen. The house is almost everywhere filled with shadowy crevices of darkness. Canyons of nostalgia and memories of rainy afternoons.

I'm sitting in a—I guess it might be called a den or a small living room. I don't know how to describe it. There's actually a formal living room off the vestibule with an adjoining dining room that leads through a door into the kitchen.

All these rooms are winter-early-afternoon-rainy dark.

I guess this room where I'm sitting writing this underneath a muted lamp has to be a den. I don't know what other room it could be. Even though it is the only room lit in the house, shadows encroach on the light.

The shadows are so close to the light that if the light were to make one slight mistake, the rainy shadows of this winter would take the room away instantly and join it with the rest of the house.

Why did it take me nine days to get back to work on this book? Should I have stayed at the hotel instead of coming back here on whatever day I returned, a day that is now in doubt of my ever actually remembering?

Was it a Sunday or a Monday?

I think I know I was here Tuesday, but if I were in court under oath, what day would I say it was?

SCENE: *A Courtroom*

I am on the stand, under oath. The judge doesn't like me. If I can be proven guilty, he will gladly give me life imprisonment without any possibility of parole. I stand accused of not knowing what day it was in February when I stopped writing this book. I am also accused of not knowing what day I moved here. The trial has gotten a lot of publicity. Jury selection was difficult. Chronologically speaking, I am considered a human monster by a lot of people who are devoted to and depend on time.

There are some people who consider time their business. They want me convicted and not let off easy.

A few other people have rallied to me, but they are considered wastrels and they obviously have not been able to mount a public protest. They have enough trouble getting anything done or getting anywhere on time, so I cannot count on their support.

My lawyer just got out of law school, where he finished at the bottom of his class. It was considered a miracle when he passed the bar because he likes to drink a lot in his spare time and professional life. There were many jokes made among his peers that that was probably the only bar that he had passed in recent years without going in and getting a drink.

It's not that I want to pass judgment upon his drinking. If I were in his place, I would probably drink, too. The ordeal of his physical extremities might drive one to drink. I don't want to go into them because I'm on the stand now being questioned by a very experienced prosecuting attorney whose father just happens to own a five-state chain of watch repair shops and a calendar factory, but I will say just one more thing about my attorney before proceeding with the trial.

My attorney is sitting beside me in the courtroom wearing a suit of armor. What drives him to drink also requires that he wear a suit of armor in public and in private.

Well, he's sort of human, too.

Why should he expose himself to something like that if he can avoid it?

Anyway, here I am on the stand and the prosecuting attorney is really pounding the questions to me. Every one of the jurors is wearing a watch prominently displayed. Some of them are wearing calendars as jewelry. Things could look better, I think, especially when I look at one of the jurors that happens to be a rabbit who has a watch obviously too big for him.

The rabbit is sneering at me.

What have I gotten myself into?

When I look at my defense attorney sitting there in the courtroom wearing a suit of armor, it doesn't make me feel any better. After the prosecution asks if I have ever lost a watch, my attorney clangs up and says, "I object! The question is not relevant to this case! The prosecution is trying to make a mountain out of a molehill!"

What in the hell does that mean?

The rabbit sneers at me and mutters under his carrot breath, "Hang the son of a bitch!" loud enough for the entire courtroom to hear.

My attorney starts to object, but the judge silences him.

"Objection overruled. Sit down before you fall down."

The suit of armor is heavy and my attorney is wobbling a little.

When he sits back down, it sounds like a garbage can full of horseshoes falling over.

What am I going to do?

Maybe we should make a deal.

I might get off with second-degree chronological negligence and be out on parole with good behavior in 1987.

I look at the rabbit.

I look at my attorney.

Would it have been a bit easier if I had picked up a calendar last month? A person doesn't think about that until something like this happens. Then it's pretty much too late.

The rabbit wants blood and it ain't carrot blood.

I don't think my attorney has the strength to stand up again. He takes something out of his briefcase, lifts up his visor, and pours it in.

> *(Exit courtroom, suit of armor, too many Goddamn watches, a bloodthirsty rabbit, and all)*

Anyway, I'm quite certain now that I was definitely living here on Tuesday last week. I know because I got a telephone call from San Francisco. It was an important call, so I remember it, which also places me here on Tuesday.

February 15, 1982 Finished.

. . . and now it's Wednesday, and I'm sitting in a coffee shop here in San Francisco, writing and still determined, well, anyway, sort of, to roughly describe what happened during the February days when I interrupted this book by not writing and moved back to the house in Berkeley where the woman hanged herself.

. . . not much really. It was a sort of drifting period of lassitude and small projects that I spent too much time doing. Two years ago I did all the things that it takes me over a week to do now in a single day of 1980.

I had no love life during the nine days, though I did have some erotic dreams. I saw some good-looking women here and there, but I was not capable of doing anything about it. A smile or a simple hello was too far beyond me.

I actually did not want the complications of meeting somebody new or seeing somebody again that I had known in the past, calling her up for lunch or dinner, and then meeting with her and having her catch me up with what had been going on in her life, and I would sit there and encourage her because I was too bored with my life to talk about it.

My life has actually been without a dynamic for over a year, and I just keep taking too long to do very simple things, and my heart has been like a colony on the moon populated by unique icicles who have apparently no transition.

I know that I have felt this way before and things have always changed when I thought that they would never change, but I still find it hard to believe that things will actually change.

It seems very hard for me to believe that I will ever start another love affair again as if from the very beginning: "Hello" to a stranger and my heart and body move toward a mutual rhythm, an involvement of styles starting their own history.

What will happen to me?

Since I have moved back to Berkeley, I have been awakened at dawn by the sound of a woman making love. I heard her again this morning . . . a soft animal moaning, but loud enough to be coming from a nearby building.

I guess that's pretty loud. The buildings here are not that close together.

She starts moaning in the dawn and perhaps it lasts for ten minutes or so. After she stops, I lie there alone in bed, so very alone in the silence of the hanged woman's covers.

Sometimes I wonder if it doesn't disturb and wake up other people who are perhaps closer to her than I am, wonder that they don't do something about it.

But what could they do?

Call the police and in turn be taken away as voyeur perverts and have their lives ruined, trying to explain to the police that this woman's screaming is waking them up and destroying their peace of mind.

So everybody keeps silent about it.

Of course she is oblivious to the knowledge that she can be heard all over the place and perhaps even further, because she would be more quiet if she knew that she was broadcasting her passion to the world.

She thinks that when she makes beautiful love in the morning it never leaves her bedroom.

She does not know that she is a part of the dawn.

February 16, 1982 Finished.

. . . suddenly it's March 1:

What happened to the last 14 days of this book, which is now obviously chronologically mischievous and grows more and more to follow the way life works out? When I started this book I promised to end it when I left for Chicago, but now I've been to Chicago and again I'm staying in San Francisco at a hotel in the Japanese section, which I guess was the ultimate destiny of these words, anyway.

It becomes more and more apparent as I proceed with this journey that life cannot be controlled and perhaps not even envisioned and that certainly design and portent are out of the question.

The process of being this book only accentuates my day-to-day helplessness. Perhaps the task I have chosen with this book was doomed from the very beginning. I should have begun with the word "delusion."

Anyway, I'm not giving up.

My trip to Chicago will not be the ending, but only

another beginning among the almost countless beginnings we have seen so far.

I left the sounds of dawn love in the strange house in Berkeley and walked down to the rapid transit train. My passage was through flowering trees to the train: apple, cherry, plum, and all in blossoms dreaming my way to Chicago.

It was cold and winter in Chicago.

There was snow on the ground.

A friend picked me up and drove me to De Kalb, Illinois, about 50 miles away, I guess. This was on February 18. I was hungry on the way, so we stopped at a McDonald's and I had a fish sandwich and a cup of coffee.

I stayed at my friend's one-bedroom apartment in a student ghetto of De Kalb, near the University of Northern Illinois, where I was to read on the 19th.

We stayed up to four o'clock in the morning drinking and catching up on current life history. Afterwards he gave me his bed and slept on the couch. My stay in his bedroom had a sort of interesting bizarreness to it that I, hopefully, will go into later. Obviously, I have not reread any of this book.

He was an English instructor at the university, and I was to teach his class that afternoon, which I did, and afterwards, I was to give an autograph party that lasted almost three hours, which I did, and I was to give a public lecture on the campus, which I did, and then go to my friend's apartment with a group of students and teachers and stay up to again 4 o'clock in the morning, which I did.

. . . and then ten days passed in the Midwest, which I did.

I will now create a system to try and sort out, and I might add in no particular order or priority other than the random selection of memory operating on its own retrieval system, some of the things that were or happened during my week and a half in the Midwest.

1.   People kept asking me why I was in the Midwest. They understood why I was there to give the lecture, but they couldn't understand why I stayed on afterwards.

"Why are you still here?" was the often question.

"I have to be someplace as long as I am alive on a planet," was the often answer.

Why did I stay on?

    a. I enjoyed the company of the people there.

    b. It was good to see my friend again, and spend some time with him.

    c. It gave me the opportunity to learn a little about the Midwest and I'm always interested in learning things.

    d. When I actually settle into a place and after a few days pass, I find it difficult to move until I have to, and then it's quite simple and often I wonder why I didn't do it before because obviously I have more than one choice of where to be, but sometimes I'm reluctant to exercise that choice if I'm already someplace else. In other words the irony here is that basically I hate to travel, even though I do a lot of traveling.

2.   I sat next to a woman at a dinner party who sold Tupperware. She was a very serious convert to Tupperware and approached the selling of it like a religion. She was also a devout worshiper of the product herself. She said that she owned over a thousand dollars' worth of Tupperware, which she had bought.

I might add something else here: She was a young college student who lived by herself and planned on never getting married.

She said that she had bought all the Tupperware as partial preparation for living the rest of her life alone. She also said when she broke up with her last boyfriend, he left Illinois and went to California and joined the Marines. So she was creating with Tupperware her own dowry to be an old maid or this was what she wanted us to believe.

What makes this all very interesting was that I didn't know what Tupperware was, and asked her to explain it to me, which for some reason was awkward for her to do. I don't think she had ever met anyone before who didn't know what Tupperware was.

I asked her about the basic unit of Tupperware. I knew that it must be a unified collection of objects and I wanted to know what thing did you start off with first.

I wanted to know about Tupperware from the very beginning.

This really confused her because she had never met anyone before who didn't know what she was talking about.

There was a professor of English sitting at the table.

Sometime during the evening, he told the dinner party that if you dropped a basketball off the top of the Empire State Building it would bounce twenty-one feet nine inches or was it seven inches into the air when it hit the sidewalk.

We could only agree with him.

I think now you can see why I spent 10 days in the Midwest. The people there are surrealistically fascinating. Often while I was listening to stuff like this, I wondered how I could possibly explain it to someone who did not live in the Midwest.

3.   During the time I spent in De Kalb, I slept in my friend's bed and he generously slept on the couch, but sleeping in his bed was uniquely interesting and provided me with another life first.

There was an apartment under his apartment, and the person in that apartment had a cuckoo clock in their bedroom which was directly underneath his bedroom, so to make a long story short, I could very distinctly hear the cuckoo clock cuckoo, when he, she, or it popped out of the clock every fifteen minutes and made a one-sound cuckoo except on the hour when it would cuckoo out the time like

> one o'clock: *cuckoo*
> two o'clock: *cuckoo, cuckoo*
> three o'clock: *cuckoo, cuckoo, cuckoo*

until the final crescending noon or midnight

cuckoo, cuckoo, cuckoo, cuckoo, cuckoo, cuckoo, cuckoo, cuckoo, cuckoo, cuckoo, cuckoo, cuckoo

The cuckoo in that clock was a really hardworking cuckoo. He, she, or it took work very seriously and was always on time. So whenever I was lying in bed awake or trying to get to sleep or waking up, my brain was assaulted by cuckoos.

Seeing that I often suffer from insomnia, I could not have dreamed up a more curious situation. When I was trying to get some sleep, just lying there in Illinois, that cuckoo regularly addled a small portion of my brain causing me to feel like a cartoon character trying to get to sleep.

I of course wondered how the person down there ever got any sleep, but I never asked to change where I slept and bed down on the couch. I knew that I would never ever sleep above a cuckoo clock again and I might as well experience it like a sort of war corespondent covering the funnies in the newspaper: byline AT THE FRONT on the funny page.

March 1, 1982 Finished.

CONTEMPORARY INTERRUPTION

I'm going to briefly interrupt this reminiscence of 1982 winter life in Illinois to write about a few things that happened here in San Francisco yesterday because one of the doomed purposes of this book is an attempt to keep the past and the present functioning simultaneously.

Yesterday was actually my first real day in San Francisco. I got back here late Saturday night from Chicago and spent Sunday getting over jet lag, which always affects me, even the two-hour time difference between Chicago and San Francisco causes my body and my senses to pay a penalty in the form of a slight disorientation, a restless weariness. I guess it even carried into yesterday.

After I finished writing, I left this little wooden table in an enclosed mall in the Japanese Trade Center, where there is a boxed tree beside the table and a couple of poinsettias sitting in the box: One of them has white leaves and the other has red leaves.

This is a quiet place to work.

It is a sort of sidewalk café, but there is no sidewalk, just the cement floors of the building surrounded by little Japanese shops and a good flow of foot traffic: tourists or Japanese people who live in San Francisco and work here or have come here to buy something or eat in one of the many restaurants in the center.

I like to look up from these words and see people walking by. This book does not require the exclusiveness of solitude.

There are two Japanese men having coffee at a table beside me.

They haven't the slightest idea what I am up to and probably would not even care. A Japanese woman just came by carrying a folded umbrella. She doesn't care either. She didn't even bother to look at me.

The reason for the umbrella: It, of course, is not raining in here, a roof and all that, but outside is different because another late winter storm wets San Francisco.

It is 8:25, this morning, and the mall is quiet and none of the shops have opened yet.

Before I wrote the last paragraph, I had planned to mention that a Japanese man at another table is eating a doughnut, but when I finished telling you what time it was and that the shops were closed, the man was gone and so was his doughnut, but just now I stared over at his absence and goddamn it, he was back again but this time had a sweet breakfast roll. When I thought he was gone, he was actually up at the restaurant counter, ordering another pastry, and was always going to return.

Yes, it is difficult to keep the past and the present going on at the same time because they cannot be trusted to act out their proper roles. They suddenly can turn on you and operate diametrically opposed to your understanding and the needs of reality.

Anyway, the reason why I guess I am turning my back on a brief stay in Illinois is to describe one thing I saw last night while walking through Chinatown to catch a bus home to the hotel.

Maybe I should have invented a different and much shorter technique to say what I wanted to say in the very beginning, which is this: I stopped at a Chinese movie theater to look at the still photographs advertising what was playing, and the films that were to come, and the next attractions included a ghost-horror movie whose horror was graphically depicted by a number of photographs showing evil ghosts and their deeds. There was also one hell-of-a poster.

An anciently-delicate, *very* old woman was standing in front of the coming-attraction window with its ghost poster and photographs, and as she looked at them she started sobbing in terror. She didn't even have to see the movie to be frightened. She was scared into tears by looking at the advertising for it. She was already sitting in her seat in the theater being frightened by a movie that wasn't going to be shown for a few days or a week.

Afterwards continuing on my way to the bus, I thought: Maybe why the advertisement for a future movie frightened her so much was because she was almost a ghost herself.

---

4.   The only tourist sight I was taken to in Illinois was the mansion that the man who invented barbed wire had built after barbed wire made him rich and famous. I can't remember his name, but we didn't go into the house, anyway. We just drove by and it was pointed out to me, and that was my extent of sight-seeing in the Midwest.

5.   Staying with my friend, we didn't do any cooking. We either ate out or consumed junk food at his place from the many franchise restaurants that abounded in the student ghetto where he lived.

Occupying a lonely outpost on the frontier of bachelor-hood, for two days straight, we ate nothing but junk food, and our role in civilization became diminished by the onslaught of hamburgers, hot dogs, take-out Italian food, fries, shakes, fish and chicken burgers until his apartment stunk with the greasy sweet pollution of junk food to the point of being an internal smog in his apartment, and after four or so junk meals, the whole place was cluttered with their leavings: greasy wax wrappers, Styrofoam boxes, empty shake and Coke cartons, decaying French fries, to the point that all the surface space in the apartment was covered with them, so we went to the next logical step in our decline and fall.

After "eating" we would take the packaging, now dismissed of "nutrient," and throw it on the floor, so that his apartment began to look like a confused picnic.

And, of course, we must not forget while this was going on, the cuckoo clock from under the bedroom floor was cuckooing out the time every fifteen minutes night and day, day and night: cuckoo.

Finally, we couldn't take it anymore and cleaned up and discarded in the garbage can our two-day museum of pop art. We had to do this because after two days of junk food, the apartment began smelling like a rapidly decomposing corpse.

Also, one of my friend's students dropped by, bringing with him a hamburger to snack on, and when the student finished the hamburger, he nonchalantly threw the Styrofoam burger box on the floor with the rest of the shit.

My friend did not think that this could lead to a meaningful student-teacher relationship.

So . . .

After all the garbage was gone and we had thoroughly aired the apartment out, so to speak exorcising it, there was a curious absence like the removal of a cartoon cancer.

6.   I met so many people that I had never met before and will never see again. That's part of traveling all the way back to here. The right now of it.

The shops in the mall are now open.

The man with the pastries who fooled my reality by doubling back on it earlier is really gone. There is not a scrap of his presence left. Except for what I have written about him on this journey there is no other evidence that he was here or even that he ever lived on this planet.

Here's a thought: What if I am lying and I just made up him and his elusive pastry eating. If I wanted a tinge of revenge, I could deny his existence entirely. He did cause me to have to dramatically alter a paragraph, which was going along more or less in a simple manner, and be forced onto a syntactical merry-go-round like trying to bail out the *Titanic* with a bucket.

But I won't abandon him to illusion.

I'll stand up, acknowledge his right to exist, though he didn't do me any great favor this morning by getting up and going for another pastry when I wasn't looking.

I wonder if he would do the same for me.

March 2, 1982 Finished.

MARCH 3, 4, 5, 6, 7, 8, 9, 10, 11, 12, 13, 14, 15, 16, 17, 18, 19, 20, 21, 22, 23, 24, 25, 26, 27, 28, 29, 30, 31 APRIL 1, 2, 3, 4, 5, 6, 7, 8, 9, 10, 11, 12, 13, 14, 15, 16, 17, 18, 19, 20, 21, 22, 23, 24, 25, 26, 27, 28, 29, 30 MAY 1, 2, 3, 4, 5, 6, 7, 8, 9, 10, 11, 12, 13, 14, 15, 16, 17, 18, 19, 20, 21, 22, 23, 24, 25, 26, 27, 28, 29, 30, 31 JUNE 1, 2, 3, 4, 5, 6, 7, 8, 9, 10, 11, 12, 13, 14, 15, 16, 17, 18, 19, 20, 21, and I now start writing again on June 22, 1982.

What in the hell happened?

Why a passage of over a hundred days between the words "I wasn't looking" and "I now start" . . . why?

What did I do in that time and where am I now?

Well, I'm a hundred days away from watching a pastry provocateur at a sidewalk café in the Japanese section of San Francisco, and I'm sitting on the back porch of my ranch in Montana where I've been since April 1 when I came up here to teach writing at a local university for the spring quarter and finished doing it 10 days ago by turning in my grades.

It's a beautiful morning here in Montana.

Every place I look it's green and sunny and birds are quite happy with it, which they show by singing and wingedly cavorting around because we had a winterlike spring here. Actually, I wouldn't even consider it a spring. The weather was so wintry with snowstorms that strained even the patience of the

most hardened Montanan causing them to become either bitter or giddy or a combination of both. They produced a sort of
Midsummer Night's surrealism.

It made the bars of Bozeman, Montana, interesting and also
the weather made it very difficult for me to get around
because somehow I had managed to break my leg in San Francisco.

I basically hate to listen to somebody's dreams and broken
leg stories fall into the same category, but people for some reason want a dramatic yarn out of a broken leg and they insist
upon it.

"How did you break your leg?" they ask eagerly, or they
pretend to be nonchalant about it. "Broke your leg, huh?"

Sure, yeah, it's broken all right.

But they won't let it go at that.

They want dramatic details and there are no dramatic
details. All broken leg stories are is being at the wrong place
at the right time, and then snap goes the calcium.

I have heard hundreds of broken leg stories.

The first time I broke my leg by stumbling over a root and
falling down a four-foot hill, that's right four feet, everybody
in San Francisco wanted to know how I broke my leg. I got so
goddamn tired of telling everybody that I stumbled over a
root and fell four feet. They always looked at me as if I weren't
telling them the truth, that I was telling them a fairy tale, so
one afternoon in a taxicab I did.

"Broken leg?" the cabby said, watching me struggle into

the cab with a pair of crutches and a cast on my leg. Those are certainly obvious clues.

"Looks like it," I said, going no further with it, and telling the driver where I wanted to go in a very precise, telegram-style form of direction. I hoped that would throw him off the scent.

I knew I had failed when he asked me where I wanted to go. I repeated my telegram of final destination and waited for *the* question.

"Broken leg?" he repeated, already set on his course. "How did you break your leg?"

"Dragon," I said.

"What?" he said, suddenly very confused now, almost rear-ending another cab. For all I know the passenger in the back-seat of that cab had a broken leg, too, and was going through the same boring ritual of repeating the same boring story he had told at least a hundred times before.

"I broke my leg stepping off a curb."

"Off the curb?"

"Off *a* curb."

"How did you do that?" the driver in front of us was asking incredulously, but not nearly as incredulous as my cabdriver was going to end up.

"I just stepped off a curb and broke it," the passenger said in front of us, looking back nervously because we had almost hit him when I said "Dragon" to my taxi driver.

"That cab's awfully close," the passenger said, fearing another broken leg from us.

"I wonder what's up his ass," the other driver said, honking and glowering back at us before probing the obvious and very boring story from his passenger also with a broken leg.

"A dragon," I repeated.

"Did you say a dragon?" my driver said.

"Yes, a dragon," I said.

"Do you mean a dragon dragon?"

"A dragon dragon," I answered, almost smiling but holding it back. The ball was now in the driver's park. Let's see what he would do with it. I had finally crossed over the point where I was not going to tell a stranger for the billionth time that I had stumbled over a root and fallen down a four-foot hill and broken my leg.

"You know what dragons are?" I asked the driver.

There was a very long silence between us as he dodged in and out of the late San Francisco rush-hour traffic. It was a three-block pause. I looked out the window and then at the back of my driver's head and into the rearview mirror where he very carefully avoided making eye contact with me.

Then he broke the silence by saying all that he was going to say during the rest of the trip.

"Yeah, I know what dragons are," he almost whispered.

So I guess what I'm trying to say is that broken leg stories are trying: very. But that still does not answer an unspoken question here that I sigh to answer *ahhhhhhhhh.* I guess that represents a sigh, reader.

—But how did you break your leg in San Francisco?—

Author: I fell over a very intelligent piece of furniture in my hotel room.

Reader: How bad was the break?

Author: It got my full attention.

Reader: How's it doing now?

Author: I'm getting around all right.

Reader: Are you still in a cast?

Author: No, they never put one on.

Reader: What? No cast. I thought you said that you broke your leg?

Author: Yeah, I broke it in two places.

Reader: Then why not a cast? What kind of break was it? Did they put a pin in it?

Author: No, the fractures were lined up perfectly and the doctor said that if I was very, very careful that I wouldn't need a cast, but I had to be very, very careful, and I was very, very careful, and now I'm getting around all right.

Reader: I have one more question.

Author: Sure, but just make sure that your question can be answered with the word "dragon."

Reader: Maybe the question isn't that important.

Author: You're sure?

Reader: Positive.

Now I'll get back to the rest of this book, whose main theme is an unfortunate woman. I'm actually writing about something quite serious, but I'm doing it in a roundabout way, including varieties of time and human experience, which even tragedy cannot escape from.

To put it bluntly: Life goes on.

Maybe Euripides woke up in the morning with a hangover while he was writing *Iphigenia in Aulis.* Perhaps funny, frustrating, totally-without-reason things happened to Euripides while Iphigenia journeyed on toward her sacrifice so the wind would come and take the Greek fleet to Troy where Ulysses picked it up from there and all the way to, years later, Ulysses returning to Ithaca and his friendly encounter with Penelope's suitors.

I wonder if she ever did any weaving after that.

June 22, 1982 Continuing . . .

Anyway, the unfortunate woman is still dead by hanging in that strange house in Berkeley where I lived for a brief time last winter. Compared to this back porch in Montana surrounded by mountains and a gathering distant electrical storm with the rumbling of approaching thunder and far-off lightning, that house seems like a dream, but her death gets no less real.

She could not stand life anymore and she hanged herself.

After 100 days of silence fell upon this notebook that I am writing in, it took only a few hours to make me feel as if I had never left.

I guess I was always here, anyway. Maybe if you return to a place, you've never really left that place because in waiting to come back, part of you is still there. If this were not true, then it would be a brand-new place, not seen before, nothing to remember it by.

And I keep remembering an unfortunate woman and what that means to all of us while thunder and lightning envision the sky here in Montana with their staging of elemental drama.

The storm is approaching, or is it slipping to the west?

I wonder how long it will be before it's here or will it ever arrive.

A wind comes up and flutters the pages of this notebook made in Japan, purchased in San Francisco, now here in Montana, containing these words and destined to end here in Montana.

. . . hopefully.

When I got this notebook to write about an unfortunate woman my plan was to end this journey when the notebook ended. There are 160 pages in this notebook. In the beginning I counted the words on each page after a day's writing. The first page has 119 words, the second 193, then 192, 168, 188, 158, 208, 167, 174, 134, 150, 142, 191, 196 *the storm is really approaching now. A strong, strong wind has come. Branches in the cottonwoods shake out and the leaves have stopped rustling and now roar like phantom lions. The thick green grass is swept by a high tide of wind. A huge bolt of lightning just flashed followed by accom-*

*panying thunder. Now another bolt of lightning but not yet the thun-
der and now the thunder. They dance to each other. A chill has come
into the air. For a few moments it was dark, but the sun is shining
briefly* 164, 167, 194, 159, 135, 233, 166, 78, and then I
stopped counting words, without even bothering to finish the
page.

I've always had at times a certain interest in counting. I
don't know why this is. It seems to come without a precon-
ceived plan and then my counting goes away. Often without
me ever having noticed its departure.

I think I counted the words on the early pages of this book
because I wanted to have a feeling of continuity, that I was
actually doing something, though I don't know exactly why
counting words on a piece of paper served that purpose
because I was *actually* doing something.

Anyway, I stopped counting words on page 22 on February
1, 1982, with a total, of 1,885 words. I hope that is the cor-
rect sum. I can count but I can't add, which in itself is sort of
interesting.

What about the storm?

Don't worry: I'll get back to it.

Just let me finish with this minor numerical theme that
arrived of its own accord and would like to finish itself. Anyway, the storm isn't doing very much right now. It's taking an
intermission.

This storm interruption just caused me to lose my train of
thought about counting or it just ended itself when it wanted

to or maybe part of what I'm trying to say is . . . I wonder how old the woman was who hanged herself. Have I been working obliquely, almost secretly, to this end.

I think she was in her early forties, but I do not know her exact age and probably never will. I guess it wouldn't make that much difference in the long run. She's very dead.

June 22, 1982 Finished.

I just stepped outside again and started writing here after a three-day absence from these pages, and I heard the distant rumble of another electrical storm.

Three days have passed.

It is now June 25, but I'm right back where I started: sitting on the porch with another electrical storm approaching.

The storm three days ago never really amounted to much. It did some medium activity and threatened a lot but it did not develop into a full storm here at the ranch. It kept its distance and then faded away into that oblivion where lightning storms retire.

I wonder if the place is like an old folks' home but instead of people, there are electrical storms wandering up and down the hall complaining about the food, "I still love my teeth. Why do I have to eat mush for dinner?" or lying silently in bed, just staring up at the ceiling until the nurse comes in and turns the senile lightning storm over, so it won't get bedsores.

Since I first came out a few moments ago, there has not been another peep out of the sky except of course for the birds. They own the sky with their voices.

Have I mentioned that there is a creek nearby and it is filled with melting snow whose original white silence in the mountains has been translated by the sun into the roar of a creek, carrying all that now noisy snow on a voyage to the Gulf of Mexico?

What was once a jewel of white silence descending in the mountain so perfect that each flake of snow was its own religion and its descent, a moving altar, is now making about as much noise as a Bowery Boys movie.

I cannot go on waiting to describe a nonexistent storm, so I will give a brief account of my morning's domesticity here at the ranch. With all the things that have gone on so far in this book, domesticity might seem rather exotic or I could talk about my love life this spring, which was sort of interesting.

I'll tell you what: I'll flip a coin to see what comes up next: a morning's domestic chores in Montana or a brief account of a love affair. I don't have a coin with me, so I'll have to go and get one in the kitchen. I'll be back in a minute and flip the coin: heads chores, tails love life.

I had been in Bozeman teaching for maybe a week when I met her. I had been drinking a lot that evening in the Bozeman bars and was feeling pretty good, even if my leg was broken in two places.

I was with some people at one of the bars and they said

there was somebody I just had to meet, that we would get along well together, also implying that she was as far-out as I was.

Sometimes I can get pretty fanciful and imaginative in my exchanges with other people. In other words: I have a reputation for being sort of wild and I guess I am. Being forty-seven years old hasn't slowed me down that much, but the other 95% of my life is very normal, quiet and often boring. People do not choose to remember that part of my life when they recount my existence on this planet.

Anyway, they called her on the telephone but she couldn't get to the bar before it closed at 2 a.m., so she would meet us at the Four B's restaurant after the bar closed, and have some coffee or breakfast with us.

The Four B's is the place where people go after the bars close in Bozeman to line stomachs with some food to help defend against the next morning's potential hangover.

I had no idea what this woman looked like except everybody said that we would like each other. That was hard for me to believe. I've never had any luck with blind dates.

Some friends once arranged a blind date for me and I got into a huge argument with my "date" at their house over her dissertation. I mean, how could this happen? I didn't even know this woman. All I wanted to do was maybe get laid or something.

Her dissertation was about Italian architecture in the novels of Henry James.

At one point the poor woman was in tears over my response to Italian architecture in the novels of Henry James.

My friends were shocked.

They had not expected Italian architecture in the novels of Henry James to turn a blind date into disaster.

But that was years ago and I found myself in a car driving toward the Four B's and in the back half of my mind wondering what I was getting myself into, but not really giving that much of a shit.

What was the possibility in this world of meeting a second blind date whose Ph.D. dissertation was on Italian architecture in the novels of Henry James?

When we pulled up at the parking lot in front of the Four B's and got out, I saw her sitting by herself in a booth, waiting for us. Even though the place was jammed with people and nobody had described her to me, I knew it was her.

I cane-hobbled over to the window and waved my free arm like a clown at her and put my face up against the glass and made clownlike motions with my features.

She was instantly delighted and started laughing.

I'm glad it was her.

I hate to think about some giant football-player type who had just gone to the toilet, returning to see this madman pressing his face up against the window terrifying his girlfriend. He might have come outside and thrown me into a snowdrift.

I am always fascinated by the physical transformation of

two complete strangers into the intimacy of lovers, lying naked beside each other silently afterwards, each with the privacy of their own thoughts, and how random and accidental this journey together is, almost like flipping a coin.

. . . heads

. . . tails

. . . and so we were lovers for the spring, sorting through the typical pleasures, misunderstandings, joys, and arguments or just sitting around for hours in the morning drinking coffee and talking about the many things there are to talk about.

She was very intelligent and so our minds could roam far and wide. Also, I find intelligence in women to be an aphrodisiac. I think I read this someplace else, but, anyway, a woman's intelligence sexually excites me.

She was one of those women who have a very good tight body but choose just to make life simpler by camouflaging it with loose-fitting clothes that lead one away from it. She didn't want to be hassled by men. She just wanted to go where she wanted to go without being an active part of a man's fantasy.

So it was very exciting to have a long conversation with her and then watch her take her clothes off. Looking back on it now, it's sort of interesting that she almost always took her own clothes off.

I think that's because she was very small, 5-2, weighing between 97 and 103 pounds, and maybe I like to take the clothes off women who are taller, but like to watch smaller women take their own clothes off.

I've never really thought much about this before and it probably would not hold up to the searchlight glare of logic because I have not been to bed recently, say in years, with a tall woman 5-7 to 6 feet, so it's hard for me to recall accurately.

I'm 6-4 and that perhaps has something to do with it, if anything does. I may be all wrong, but it seems to me that it's easier to take the clothes off a tall woman, the somewhat equal closeness of her eyes watching my eyes, but with a short woman it's so far down to her eyes and looking up she has to strain her head or maybe it causes an awkwardness to occur in me taking her clothes off.

Maybe the bending over does it.

I don't know. I'll have to bed with a tall woman one of these days to see if this hypothesis has any verity, but this book I'm afraid will be over before anything is proved one way or another.

I did have a chance to go to bed with a tall woman last week.

We talked for a couple of hours, and running out of things to say, at one point I asked her how tall she was.

"5-10" was the reply.

I wonder if I would have taken her clothes off, if things had ever gotten that far. She did have interesting-looking breasts and a small waist. The blouse she was wearing would have come off quite easily and I would have been looking into her eyes and it would have not been any effort for her to have looked into my eyes.

I wonder . . .

There's also something else that I just remembered that plays a part in my love life. Often I like to take my clothes off and get into bed first and lie there and watch the woman take her clothes off, and how she does it.

Sometimes they do it very quickly and as fast as they take off a garment, they just drop it on the floor and then almost jump into bed when they are finished.

Other women take their clothes off very slowly and carefully, then fold them neatly on a chair or whatever is about before gliding like a swan into bed.

I might add that whatever way a woman chooses to take her clothes off does not have anything to do with the quality of her lovemaking.

. . . and there is of course something else.

Perhaps this resembles an erotic spice and a spying glass into my mind and its sensuality. Sometimes I like to spend an entire night staying up talking with a woman in the front room, drinking whiskey and talking until dawn or almost, and sometimes during those nights, I'll suddenly ask, interrupting whatever is being talked about, either a movie or the precarious fate of the American novel or perhaps a story about a boring mutual friend who's so boring that we have to talk about them for at least an hour, and then suddenly I ask the woman to take her clothes off.

I usually word it this way, "Please take your clothes off," and usually the woman does it without saying a word about it and we continue talking about the boring friend while she takes her clothes off.

After she has them off, we continue talking as if she still had her clothes on, and I make no romantic overtures toward her. I just want to see her with her clothes off because I enjoy the sight of her body. It adds to the whiskey and the conversation. The women never seem to mind and act perfectly natural. They curl up on a couch and the night moves on. If I see they are getting cold, I find a blanket for them and turn up the heat.

Sometimes after they are warm and cozy under the blanket and the room is hot enough, I interrupt whatever we are talking about. We have of course finished with the boring friend and are on to something else. Maybe we are talking about the morality of suicide.

I interrupt by saying, "Let me see your breasts," and the woman exposes her breasts without a break in the conversation, acting as if it is the most natural thing in the world for me to want to see her breasts while we are talking about suicide.

There has probably been a question that you have wanted to ask almost from the beginning of this little revelation of mine.

I have trouble with the word "kinky" because frankly I have difficulty understanding that word. There once was an English woman who lived in the 19th century who said the best thing I've ever heard about one's sexual preference or activity.

She said something like "I don't care what anyone does, just as long as they don't do it in the street and frighten the horses."

I know that is not the exact quote but it is close enough for my purpose. Maybe in this time we could substitute motorcycles for horses.

Yes, back to the real question that you have wanted to ask me.

"Do you take your clothes off?"

"No."

"Why not?"

"Because it's not the effect that I want to produce. I enjoy the sight of a woman's body at play in the fields of intelligence."

"What if things were reversed and the woman asked you to take your clothes off while she left hers on, would you do it?"

"Of course."

I'll end this day's writing by saying that the electrical storm never materialized, one more for the old folks' home.

June 25, 1982 Finished.

Today starts with me talking to a friend on the telephone last night.

Oh, yes, we're on the same back porch with no electrical storm in sight and the sun and the birds shining away in the sky and a few white clouds billowing about, seeming almost to be reflections coming off the snow in the mountains to the west, which go steplike miles to the Pacific Ocean far away and where I talked to a friend last night.

I called him, thinking that he might be in a good mood. He normally has a few drinks by the time I call him in the evening, and for some reason I thought he might be in a cheerful mood and we could share a few laughs.

I was very wrong.

I should learn never to trust my intuitions. I wonder why at 47 I still persist in doing so, but it was much too late after he answered.

He was in the worst mood I had ever heard him in. It was as if the elevator of hell had gone crashing through his life, making an elevator-shaped hole in his spirit.

Soon he was weeping.

I listened very carefully and understandingly to what no person ever wants to hear, which they do not need to hear. It does them no good and generates a huge vacuum of helplessness.

What could I do? Except to be his friend and listen . . . and listen . . . and listen . . . and listen . . . and listen until the act of listening dropped an elevator of hell through my soul.

You would need some strange meter, perhaps designed by Kafka, to measure who felt worse now: him or me. The dial, if there were a dial on Kafka's meter, would probably register our lives at just about almost identical readings.

I tried to tell him to look on the bright side, funny, huh?

and things would change, and then I continued listening . . . and listening . . . and listening. At times his voice became my voice and then we exchanged voices back again.

The fears, doubts, and self-tragedies that he spoke of were all things that had haunted me for many years and were shared parts of my darkness, things that I had to conceal to go on living. They were things that sometimes escaped from the prison I held them in myself. They would either ingeniously escape like a perfect prison break or I would just simply open the cell door for them to come out and tear the living shit out of me like rabid werewolves often in the middle of the night when I was alone and there was no one to turn to and the only defending silver bullet was on a side of the moon that was so dark that it would make 1930s Shirley Temple tap-dancing seem like coal growing slowly, painfully over millions of years in the gardens beneath the ground.

Often when I was listening to him, I thought that we were talking at the same time, saying exactly the same things like a chorus of coal.

He was by now very, very drunk and often wept over the telephone.

I shared everything with him but the weeping. I would have plenty of time for that later on soon, approaching soon when a friend of mine would die of cancer.

His weeping was now the main feature.

My weeping would be another movie.

My time would come when she died.

So now I could share every darkness with my friend except for the weeping.

At the end of the conversation I had him get a piece of paper and a pencil. I told him some elemental things to do. First, I told him to write down the date June 25th and the words "Conversation between RB and CN." I had him make a list: 1 to 5, because I thought that he was so drunk that he would forget our conversation by the time he woke up in the morning and stared exhaustedly around his apartment, wondering what had happened last night after drinking so much whiskey that he had passed out, and perhaps wondering if he had talked to somebody on the telephone and who it was and what they talked about or maybe not even thinking about that at all, just staring at the morning light near the Pacific Ocean and then returning to an elevator falling through a slowly growing coal field, far from the surface of the earth.

"Do you have the paper and the pencil?"

"Yes," *slurred*.

"I want you to write the number one."

"One?" *slurred*.

"Yeah, one."

"OK," *slurred*.

"Now write down the word 'eat' after one."

He had told me that he hadn't eaten in three days. His normal weight is 150 pounds. I had asked him how much he weighed now and he'd said, "one hundred and twenty pounds. I can't eat anymore. The thought and smell of food makes me nauseous." Then he had told me that for three days he had been living off of drinking chocolate milk, Gatorade, and 100 proof whiskey, and he would wake up at 10:30 in the morning and start drinking whiskey at 11:30.

"Eat?" he *slurred*.

"After the number one, write 'eat.'"

"I can't make out my own handwriting. What did you just ask me to write?"

"E-A-T."

June 26, 1982 Finished.

. . . and it's tomorrow in the late afternoon and another electrical storm threatens. Just now as I started to write, some thunder roared a few miles away to the west, and the creek continues to roar its bank-filled snow down to the Yellowstone River.

Yesterday after I finished writing about my friend's contagious darkness, I went over to Bozeman and spent the night drinking to forget a week full of problems, my own and my friends'. There are more than enough problems to go around right now.

I am haunted by the woman who is dying of cancer. I talked to her on the telephone the same night I was joined to my friend's darkness. I had sent her a telegram last week. I hoped that it would make her feel peaceful. It's a little late to send a get-well card. She now has a private telephone in her hospital room.

She answered the telephone with a voice that was very delicate, a gentleness that had never been in her voice before. She sounded as if she had to walk across a bridge to use the telephone or maybe the telephone was at one end of the bridge and she was at the other end, using it across the distance with an extension cord of dying.

I guess what I'm trying to say is that her voice was gently clear like a small candle burning in an immense darkened cathedral built for a religion that was never finalized, so no worship ever took place in there.

She told me how much she liked the telegram, how beautiful it was, and I must write more things like it to her, and then again she said how beautiful it was.

What I said in the telegram was this:

WORDS ARE FLOWERS OF NOTHING. I LOVE YOU

"It made me feel good," she said. "It was beautiful. Please write me more."

I have to stop writing this book for a few moments while I go up and check around the barn for a lost kitten. A neighbor came by a few days ago and told me that they had lost a kitten and would I please look for it. I think I've been hearing cat noise up by the barn.

At first I wasn't certain, and I'm still not, but I'll go check, anyway. Back in a moment. . . .

No kitten, but I did jump a whitetail deer that had been lying in the high grass within twenty-five feet of me down in some old abandoned corrals that are memories of the 19th century. I said "Kitty, kitty, kitty, kitty," one time too many and the deer got up and jumped over the railing of the corral.

The deer was a beautiful whitetail buck and sailed effortlessly over what man built a long time ago. I think the men who built that corral are now in the local cemeteries.

The thunder stopped for a while and now it's starting up again, and the air all around is filled with drifting cottonwood seeds. They blow up onto the porch where I write.

They just really started today.

They resemble late June abstract snow.

I remember two years ago in 1980, they were blowing around like this before I went down to Colorado, where I embarked on an extraordinary love affair with a brilliant young poetic Japanese woman.

She is now back in Japan, where she writes me haunting letters which try to evoke my emotions, which curiously come and go, leaving me disturbed and perplexed. I wonder if our involvement is over or moving into a different stage.

I wonder if I will ever see her again except perhaps only in photographs. I saw a photograph taken of her two years ago when she came up from Colorado to visit me here in Montana. Some friends took the photograph and they showed it to me for the first time a few weeks ago.

In the photograph she is standing with her long black hair and delicately cute, pouty face beside the Firehole River in Yellowstone National Park.

She was twenty-three years old then, but she looked fifteen.

Now she is twenty-five and I am forty-seven.

That's a lot of years difference. Sometimes she kids me in her letters saying that we should see each other soon before I am a very old man.

I wonder what will happen.

There is a deer in the backyard, standing in front of the corrals. It's about a hundred feet away, staring at me.

While I was paying attention to the Japanese woman, the deer silently, completely unnoticed, slipped in, and when I just looked up from this sentence, the deer was slipping out of sight back to the same place my "Kitty, kitty, kitty, kitty" disturbed it from a little while ago.

The way that deer is moving spylike around I wouldn't be surprised to look over right now and find it sitting in the chair next to me here on the porch with its own notebook and pen writing things down.

I think the reason for the voice change in my friend who is dying of cancer was because of sedation, and also, I think she is growing to accept the idea of her own death.

At first she was very frightened when she told me that she had cancer. She has always been a very strong, purposeful woman with a very dynamic and aggressive personality. Cancer had reduced her to a frightened crying little girl, but when I talked to her a few nights ago, she was delicate, calm. I think she is now getting used to the idea of dying. She did not mention her illness to me, other than to say that she was feeling better. She said it very casually, almost matter-of-factly.

Yes, I think she is getting used to the idea of her own death.

Anyway, the telephone calls took place on Friday and now it is Sunday just two days later, though it seems like a much longer time to me.

Maybe weeks . . .

. . . and I went to Bozeman yesterday to try and forget all about it by doing some drinking and perhaps meeting a woman and what follows that.

I need a little loving, too, sometimes.

But all that happened was that I did a lot of drinking and then walked three-quarters of a mile alone after the bars closed to a cheap motel room that rented for $9.95 a night, very modest and clean.

It was just a little too long a walk for my fractures, and so today, I've had to favor my leg, and I fell into bed last night very terribly alone.

This morning I came back to Livingston in a yellow school bus driven by a friend going to pick up a group of children who had spent a week at a camp up in the mountains behind my place, so he was going to be driving right by my house.

I had never been the only passenger on a school bus before.

My friend very generously stopped at a grocery store in Livingston, so I could get provisions for a week's stay out here by myself. I lingered in the produce section for a while and got a lot of stuff for making salads, which I haven't been eating very much of recently.

Then I bought a couple of bottles of prepared salad dressing.

When the checker was adding up my food at the counter, suddenly without even being really conscious that I was speaking out loud, I said, "I think I'll eat a lot of salads this week."

"Excuse me?" the checker said, thinking that I was talking to him and of course not understanding what I was talking about. How was one to understand "I think I'll eat a lot of salads this week" right out of the clear blue?

"Nothing," I said. "I was just thinking out loud."

The checker did not pursue it.

. . . and as I finish this day's writing, again a threatening electrical storm did not materialize and I'm off to bed early tonight, sleeping in my own bed. Right now I have a lot of difficulty believing that I woke up this morning in a $9.95 motel room in Bozeman.

It's almost as if I had never left here yesterday, looking for love as they say in all the wrong places. Maybe I did this three weeks ago and just lost track of time. That seems closer to the truth.

June 27, 1982 Finished.

June 28, another day in my life, begins here right now at 9:30 in the morning, but strangely enough there is no threatening storm, and no roar of distant thunder, all to develop into nothing.

There is of course the sound of the creek that will not go away as it continues to journey snow out of the mountains. Birds are singing. The sun is shining with wispy clouds blowing about.

Maybe a non-storm will show up later in the day.

Flowers are blooming everywhere but the cottonwood seeds are absent from the view. Not one of them floats like abstract snow across this page.

I think what I did last night is the opposite of abstract snow. I made a huge vat of spaghetti sauce late in the evening. Actually, I made it too late to be considered dinner.

I couldn't think of anything else to do.

A friend called me up on the telephone a few days ago and excitedly told me that he had just come across an excellent TV set for only forty dollars. It was a nineteen-inch black-and-white. I didn't have a TV set. I had one, but it died last year.

"You say it's in excellent condition?" I asked. My experience with cheap used black-and-white sets has not been good. They are usually 99/100% dead but just haven't fallen over yet. They are waiting for some poor deluded sap who thinks that there is perhaps six months or maybe even a year left in it, and then the TV drops dead.

"It's in perfect condition," my friend said. "I've tried it out."

My friend knows a little about electronics, so I said yes, and the next day the television set was in my house. It took a little time to adjust the picture because my aerial isn't hooked up.

Then I had a picture and my friend went on his way.

I could now take a peek at the world beyond the mountains.

I could watch the evening news and be right up to the moment in watching the world go to hell, and not feel left out.

I didn't turn the set on until yesterday afternoon and then I was watching a news program, finding out exactly what was going on in the world . . . for 6 minutes before the picture started acting crazy and jerking around in the typical death throes of a dying TV set.

I divided my cash output, $40.00, into my total viewing time on the set, 6 minutes, and came up with a per-minute cost of $6.66. If I had watched that set for an hour before it died, I could have bought a brand-new set with the money it would have cost me.

So I guess I got off easy with 6 minutes of being a TV viewer.

Anyway, I had nothing to occupy myself with last night, so I made a huge pot of spaghetti sauce starting from scratch, slicing onions, mushrooms, a green pepper, etc. I put olives in my sauce and went and got a tin of them I bought a month ago. When I bought them, I thought they were pitted, so I planned on slicing them up for the sauce as I headed in the direction where I keep my canned food.

I easily found the olives, and surprise!

They had changed in one month from pitted olives to olives with their pits still in them. That's quite a feat, bordering on a miracle.

My spaghetti sauce was completed at a quarter of eleven.

That's very late to cook spaghetti, not unless you own a restaurant, but it had filled up my evening, and was not costing me $6.66 a minute. There was of course a simple plan behind cooking the sauce so late. I was going to freeze it into one-helping plastic bags and eat off the sauce for weeks to come.

In the last cooking stages of spaghetti, I went into the front room and read a biography of William Faulkner. It's a two-volume biography and I read it from time to time, mostly when I'm depressed.

I guess I was depressed making the spaghetti sauce because I was reading the life of William Faulkner. I admire William Faulkner's work very much, but his life was depressing while my spaghetti bubbled away in the kitchen with ripped-apart olive fragments as a part of it.

Oxford, Mississippi.

June 28, 1982 Continuing . . .

Back again: 10 of 12 and still morning and with the warmth of the sun, there are gusts of abstract snowflakes in the air, every cottonwood flake wanting to be a tree. During the time I was gone, I ate some of my nocturnal spaghetti, read the day's incoming mail delivered at 10:30 to a blue mailbox in front of my house.

The mail was pleasant enough.

Then I went to a neighbor's house across the creek and got a glass of vodka. My neighbor is gone on a trip but the person taking care of their house kindly gave me a glass of vodka.

I drank it and returned to this place where we have been meeting sporadically since January 30 of this year. That seems like so long ago, but for two years now time, experience, and emotions have been stretched out, elongated to a point that a dozen years seem to have passed and more experiences and emotions than could be counted by all the computers in Japan operating simultaneously.

A wind has come up and it is now roaring in the top branches of the cottonwood trees that send forth their parachute seeds, questing for life. All the branches in all the trees are turning about, and every blade of grass and each flower bows to the wind.

I find myself now here in Montana describing so much weather, so much actual change or change that threatens to occur but does not. I wonder if I am also describing myself. I think I said something in the beginning of this book about it being a kind of brief calendar map of my own journey through life.

Also, I am always the last person to know what's going on in my life, but I have a feeling that's maybe the way it is with everybody and belief in self-understanding is only a delusion. I wonder if I am beginning to sound like Gibran's *The Prophet*.

One of the letters I got today was from my daughter. It was a Father's Day card. She is twenty-one and lives in the East.

She got married last year and I disapproved of the marriage and things have been strained ever since then between us. I know it has been hard on her but it has also been very hard on me because I love her very much. We'll just have to let enough time pass to solve this one. She and I were very close until she got married. Now our communication is minimal and strained.

Perhaps I should bend a little.

I don't know.

I still disapprove of the marriage.

She called me on the telephone a week ago Sunday to wish me a happy Father's Day. We'd had no communication since November. We did not acknowledge each other on Christmas, my birthday, or hers. The telephone seems to be playing a large part in my life these days. It was not a pleasant conversation. We talked around things that may take years for us to talk about in the open.

I went into too much detail about my teaching this spring. She listened patiently for about fifteen minutes, probably bored. Then she told me what she was doing with her life, not talking about certain things, talking around things.

I *was* bored, even though she took only a few minutes to tell me her story.

When at last we had filled up the space for a Father's Day telephone call and our first conversation since November, about eight months ago, it was now time for one of us to initiate hanging up.

One of the things that we did not talk about was when we

would see each other again. She knew that I would not want to see her in the immediate or longer than that future with her husband either in New York or out here in Montana. I cannot invite her to visit me because of the awkwardness that would be created by omitting that her husband come.

I initiated the closing down of the conversation by saying, "Well, I guess we've spent enough time talking on your dime."

"I guess so," she said.

Now the stopwatch was running out on the last minute of our first contact in eight months. There was a pause while some more seconds instantly dried up like rubbing alcohol.

Meanwhile the question: When would we see each other again? hung in the electrons between an isolated telephone in Montana and the capital of American energy New York.

Finally, she said, "We'll have to have lunch sometime."

I answered by saying that I might be in New York sometime in December or later next year, maybe the spring. I had been invited to France and would probably stay in New York on my way over or back. Maybe if our schedules coincided we could get together.

The telephone call was over shortly after that.

I felt very disturbed and wished that she had never called me.

I stared at the telephone, betrayed again by this strange instrument so far removed from nature. I've never seen anything in nature that looked like a telephone. Clouds, flowers, rocks, none of them resemble a telephone.

I don't know what's going to happen between my daughter and me. I've searched through the possibilities like an archaeologist. These ruins puzzle and haunt me. But I haven't the slightest idea how to catalog them and what museum they will end up in and if the dig has just begun or is it over.

June 28, 1982 Continuing . . .

All I know is that there is nothing quite as destructive, distracting, and ultimately stupid as family warfare, but it's so hard to gain any objectivity about declaring a truce and peace to return to the land.

I have seen so many family feuds burn out of context like forest fires until the landscape is nothing but ashes.

Then what?

I guess it's time for a break right now. I think I'll go get a glass of wine and walk around a bit. There's an old abandoned junk car right beside the barn. Sometimes I like to sit down on the hood and lean up against the windshield like sitting on a couch, and stare at the snowy mountains a few miles to the east.

Maybe I'll go do that and watch the silence of the snow in the mountains that will be roaring in the creek by my house in a few days.

Yeah, that's a good idea.

It wasn't really that good of an idea because the temperature is close to 80, and the sun is really beating down on the car, sort of barbecuing it on a summer day.

It was almost too hot to sit down on, but I sat down couch-like on it anyway for a few minutes, then I realized that I didn't have a hat or a long-sleeved shirt on, and being very fair, and at this altitude, around 5,000 feet, I'd be cooking along with that car very shortly, so I came back.

There are a few things intelligence is good for, not damn many, but a few. Before I went up to the car, I got a glass of wine as I said I would—interruption for a Montana nature break. I just felt something dimly crawling on my arm, the one away from this pen, and saw a very, very, very tiny orange spider crawling along the top of the hair on that arm.

I am very hairy in a blond way. A few times women have told me that they were sexually attracted to the hair on my body. Needless to say, I could never figure that one out.

The spider is now relaxing on one particularly long blond hair. I have not moved my arm since I first discovered him there because I have not had to turn a page. He remains on me as I remain on this page, but I will have to turn it over soon because I am running out of space. I wonder where in the fuck the spider thinks he is. He's almost taking a rest. Maybe he plans on building a web and taking up residency on my arm.

OK, I just turned the page, moving my arm to do so, but it had no effect on him. Maybe he thinks I'm a branch in a tree and my movement is just the movement of the wind.

He's very still now, curled up at the end of the hair.

I do believe he is asleep.

No, he just woke up and started running all over the place which happens to be my arm. As you have probably already surmised, spiders do not make me squeamish.

He sure is small. He's about four times bigger than a period. Goddammit, he is spinning a web! I think I've had enough of this. Not being afraid of spiders is one thing, but spinning webs and planning to take up living on you is another.

I'm going to get rid of this little guy.

I'm going to step off the porch and blow him off my arm, so he can find a new place to live. This is one of those times when a 30-day eviction notice is not necessary.

I wish him all the luck in the world and then blow him off my arm into the grass of the backyard, ultimately a better place to live than on my arm. I think the first time I took a shower with him at home on my arm with perhaps a few insects about the size of two periods in his web, it would be an irrevocable experience for him.

Where was I before I noticed the spider setting up housekeeping on me? Oh, yes, I didn't go directly to the car after pouring myself a glass of wine. I walked over to my neighbors' house to see if they had gotten back from a month-long trip back East. They had called the person who was taking care of their house and told them that they had left Chicago by automobile yesterday morning and would be here today.

Well, I walked over to their place after getting the glass of wine and nobody was there. They had not gotten in yet from Chicago and the person who had given me the vodka was also gone, so I walked back home, pausing on the bridge across the creek to stare at the water-powered snow roaring along.

I don't know if I mentioned that little trip the first time or not. It's not really very important. Then I went up to the barbecuing car and sat down on the hood and stared at the mountains. I paid particular attention to a couple of mountains where the snow was framed against trees and rocks and blue sky.

I was looking at the snow that would soon be expressing itself down the creek. I wondered if it had any idea of its fate and the trip down to the Gulf of Mexico, that soon it would become Pine Creek and then part of the Yellowstone River, to join the Missouri, then get involved with the Mississippi and flow past Natchez and eventually the smell of creole cooking would drift across its now familiarized watery nostrils.

Sitting on the hood of that car staring at the snow in the Absaroka Mountains, I knew that it didn't have the slightest idea that it would become acquainted with gumbo.

The car I was sitting on had a sort of interesting brief history. A couple of teenage boys drove it up from Texas in 1978 and something went wrong with it in Denver. The thing that went wrong with the car can only be described in beautiful American colloquial English: "The engine blew up."

The boys bought another car in Denver and towed this one

to the place right beside the barn where it has stayed ever since. They worked on it a little, got homesick, and went back to Texas, leaving me with a perfect automobile couch.

June 28, 1982 Continuing...

This day's writing seems to be written almost in strophes. I have been away from here for the last half an hour. I needed a break to sort of gather my thoughts as I see that we are very close to the end of this journey. I rattle on about abandoned cars, spiders, a perhaps abnormal fascination with melting snow, but all the time I continue using up the few remaining pages in this notebook.

During my half-an-hour departure, I talked to a former writing student of mine this spring. She is quite talented and wants to know what to do because she really enjoys writing.

She is eager to learn.

We talked on the telephone about a story of hers that did not go well and talked about what went wrong with it. I told her that she was writing too far away from her own experience and that in this stage in her writing, she has only been writing for little more than a year, she should stay a little closer to the things that she knows until she has the technical tools to make a bridge, a longer bridge, away from her own life.

In other words, I told her to write about the things she knows about.

There would be plenty of time to write about what she doesn't know about.

So I now find myself bringing to an end this book, which is basically about all I know about, so painfully evident. If I am to be trusted, and writers are notorious liars, I will say now that the only rereading of this book was to find out where I was when I stopped writing and lapsed into so many short and painfully embarrassing longer lapses.

At this point you know more about what has gone on now than I do. You have read the book. I have not. I of course remember things in it, but I am at a great disadvantage right now. I am literally in the palm of your hand as I finish.

Of course the last week's writing is familiar to me, but I am uncertain as to parts that occurred before the long exile that happened in which I did not write. It is between then and now that is my greatest concern as I finish.

Because my plan was to write a book following like a calendar map the goings-on of my life. I can't return to the beginning and what followed after that. I wish I could. It would make things a lot easier. I know there are so many loose ends, unfinished possibilities, beginning endings.

If I could only turn back right now and gather a bunch of them together, but I'm not going to. I will finish as I started toward no other end than a human being living and what can happen to him over a given period of time and what if anything, it means.

I sense this book to be an unfinished labyrinth of half-asked questions fastened to partial answers.

What about the unfortunate woman who hanged herself? Where have I left her? Is she now some kind of forgotten ornament suspended in eternity? What was her childhood like? Did I go into the reason why she hanged herself? Do I even really know? Remembering back to the beginning, I started off with a lone woman's shoe lying in a Honolulu intersection. So what . . . ?

Will my daughter and I ever get together?

I think I wrote something about pastry.

Was it meant to be funny?

What about the lovers I mentioned in this book?

Where are they now?

Why am I out here alone.

My friend continues to die of cancer, even as I write now shardlike cells grow inside of her, never stopping until I talk about her only in the past tense.

What about the student who wants to write? Stay home, I say, knowing that this book has been my home, not often visited but still my home, since the day of my 47th birthday, and my stupid broken leg, and it seems to me that I wrote something about chickens in this book, and Alaska, and Chicago, and Canada, and all the tumbled machinations that are a man's mind and his experience.

I am haunted, almost obsessed, by all the things that I have left out of here, that needed at least equal time, who is to champion their cause as with each stroke of my pen I consume this space, precious perhaps only to me, but precious, anyway.

Why did I spend time writing about electrical storms that

never happened when I could have been delving more understandingly, compassionately, into the woman who hanged herself?

What about all the things that are not here and how little did I do with what is here?

So many inconclusive fragments, sophomoric humor, cheap tricks, detailless details.

Why did I waste so much of these 160 pages in a notebook costing me $2.50 bought in a Japanese bookstore on my birthday? See, I'm doing it again. Perhaps I'm a helpless case and should accept my fate. With so little space left, I'm writing about how much this goddamn notebook cost.

I can't believe it.

I just can't believe it.

I think I'll pause to see if I can believe it.

I'm going to get up and walk around this Montana landscape for a little bit. A terrible sadness is coming over me. I'll be back in a while to make this book gone.

I'm back.

Oh, I went for a little walk over to my neighbors, not home, and back across the creek again, snow, etc. Speaking of snow, of course we were all talking about snow, I just emptied the ice-cube tray in the freezer into an ice-holding container and refilled the tray with water, which happens to come from the creek. That's where I get my water, so the snow just recently up in the mountains is now in my freezer to be refrozen into different-shaped flakes, nice in a glass of whiskey.

I'm now starting the last page (160) of this book. There are 28 lines to a page and I write on every other line, so I can add things in between the lines if I want to. That's 14 writing lines to a page times 160.

Yeah, that's what it is.

I can't help but smile right now. You'll have to admit it is sort of funny. There are ten writing lines left on this page and I have decided not to use the last line. I'll leave it to somebody else's life. I hope they will make better use of it than I would have.

But I did try.

My thanks to the JMPC Company of Japan for printing this notebook and for the Kinokuniya bookstore in San Francisco for importing it. I also thank the Pilot Pen company of Japan for manufacturing two Pilot BP-S pens who were my two other companions on this calendar closed now like a door.

June 28, 1982

☐

"Iphigenia, your daddy's home from Troy!"